NANCY WARREN

PURLS AND POTIONS

VAMPIRE KNITTING CLUB
BOOK FIVE

D0863202

ISBN: ebook 978-1-928145-53-0

ISBN: print 978-1-928145-54-7

Cover Design by Lou Harper of Cover Affair

Ambleside Publishing

INTRODUCTION

Lucy's first love potion goes horribly wrong
Romances get tangled
But worse, someone dies!

Romance is in the air on Harrington Street, Oxford. Detective Inspector Ian Chisholm is finally showing interest in Lucy, though the members of the vampire knitting club aren't too thrilled to have the police hanging around so close to Cardinal Woolsey's yarn shop. Up the street at Frogg Books, shop assistant Alice is in love with her bookish boss, Charlie, who doesn't seem to notice.

Lucy's trying to become more proficient as a witch and when her cousin Violet talks her into brewing up a love potion to bring Alice and Charlie together, it seems like a harmless way to improve her craft.

Until someone dies. Is Lucy's love potion more deadly than cupid's arrow? Or is there a killer on the loose?

The best way to keep up with new releases and special

offers is to join Nancy's newsletter at **nancywarren.net** or her Facebook readers group, Nancy Warren's Knitwits. www.facebook.com/groups/NancyWarrenKnitwits

PURLS AND POTIONS

CHAPTER 1

*F*rogg's Books on Harrington Street was exactly what a bookshop ought to be. The walls were lined with floor-to-ceiling bookshelves displaying novels, both popular and literary, non-fiction suitable for both Oxford students and the casual reader, and a colorful selection of children's titles. Cozy armchairs were tucked in quiet corners, inviting the customer to sit and browse.

It was across the street and up the block from Cardinal Woolsey's, the knitting and yarn shop I owned in Oxford. My cousin, and part-time shop assistant, Violet, and I walked up on that February morning with a definite purpose in mind.

We wanted to recruit Alice Robinson, the bookstore assistant, to come and teach knitting classes in my shop. I'd have taught them myself except that I was probably the worst knitter who ever owned a knitting shop. Vi could knit, but she claimed she couldn't teach.

Alice seemed like an excellent choice in a knitting teacher. She was soft-voiced, kind and turned out beautiful work. I'd been exposed to the best, since I was so often the recipient of the gorgeous sweaters, shawls, coats and scarves knitted by my friends in the vampire knitting club that met in the back room of my shop. Still, for a living woman who hadn't had hundreds of years to perfect her craft, Alice was pretty darned good with the needles.

Also, she was nice. I'd had some shady characters end up in my shop and what I liked about Alice was that she didn't seem to be a soul-sucking demon, a murderer, or a thief. Excellent qualifications in someone working with the public.

I'd wanted to offer knitting classes to patrons with a pulse for sometime now but I'd needed to find the right teacher. Since discovering that Alice had taught at her last job, in a knitting shop in Somerset, I'd been keeping an eye on her. Sure, I didn't want to steal the assistant out from under the nose of Frogg's Books owner, Charlie Wright but, frankly, Charlie so rarely saw what was under his nose that I doubted he'd notice if she stopped coming in.

Violet and I were doing some undercover sleuthing, feeling out whether Alice might be amenable to teaching classes one evening a week and on Sunday afternoons. If she worked out, she'd earn some extra money and get an excellent discount on anything she purchased from Cardinal Woolsey's.

We walked into the bookstore and I took a moment to look around. I loved the colorful displays of wool in Cardinal Woolsey's, a patchwork of rainbow shades that made actual knitters long to buy patterns and wool and get started.

I felt the same longing when I came in here. The books all called to me, begging to be read. If I had time, I'd curl up in the empty armchair in the corner with a brand new novel and read a few pages before taking it home with me.

There were a couple of people browsing. Charlie Wright was at the counter near the back of the shop. It was the cash desk and his work area. He was seated, reading a book. I suspected he read every single volume that came through his door, sublimely unconscious of customers, noise, or boxes to be unpacked.

I knew he was thirty-four, because he'd told me when we'd chatted at the most recent meeting of our local shop owners' association. As far as I knew, he'd never been married. Like me, he lived in the flat above his shop, though I suspected his was quieter than mine, since I lived above a nest of vampires, including my grandmother, who often came to visit in the evenings.

He appeared to be a man whose friends were his books. He had thick, dark hair that flopped down on his forehead as he bent over reading. He turned a page and pushed his reading glasses up onto the bridge of his nose with his index finger.

He wore a pink shirt, though it was that shade of pink you get from absent-mindedly putting something white into the wash with something red.

Alice was unpacking a box of novels onto the display table at the front of the shop. She was doing a Valentine's Day theme, so they were all love stories, both classic and modern. She wore her dark hair French braided and then coiled at the back, though a few wispy ringlets managed to escape and curl around her heart-shaped face. She had clear gray eyes behind large glasses, a straight nose and full lips. I'd never seen her wear cosmetics.

She hand-knitted her own cardigans and sweaters and while the work was exquisite, I always felt that she knitted the pattern one or two sizes larger than necessary. This meant that all her sweaters were baggy, so she must have liked them that way. Under her sweaters she wore crisp blouses done up to the neck and longish woolen skirts with sensible low-heeled shoes. She looked like a combination between a schoolgirl and a middle-aged matron.

I guessed her to be about five years older than my own twenty-seven. Unlike the shop's owner, she'd glanced up when the bell rang announcing new customers. She put down the books she was unpacking, in a neat stack on the table, and came forward with a smile. "Lucy. Violet. How nice to see you. Are you looking for anything special or just browsing?"

She had a clear, pleasant voice and there was something comfortable about her. I knew she was the perfect choice to teach my beginner's class. I was very keen to get a good teacher as I planned to take the class myself.

"I want to talk to you," I said, "Whenever you have a minute."

She glanced around. "We're not that busy. How can I help you?"

Her face softened when she looked at Charlie Wright. No doubt she believed her feelings were known only to herself, but everyone in the neighborhood knew she was in love with Charlie. Everyone except Charlie himself.

I was extra sensitive to people's feelings, being a witch, but her yearning was so strong I could hear it, like a soulful sigh.

I explained to her that I was starting classes and I wanted her to teach them. She seemed taken aback by the idea and turned her gaze from Charlie to me. "Oh, I don't know. I'm very busy here."

I emphasized the hefty store discount and that we could work around Frogg's schedule.

"I don't know. I like to be available, in case Charlie needs me."

I wanted to tell her to stop being a doormat, to accept that Charlie treated her like an old and comfortable pair of slippers. But I understood a little bit about unrequited love and so I kept my peace. "Talk it over with Charlie and let me know," I said.

"Yes. Yes, I will. And thank you for asking me." Since we were there anyway, I decided to buy one of the novels Alice was unpacking. It looked like a very satisfying love story. Vi, meanwhile, wandered around the non-fiction shelves, emerging with a book about local herbs.

By that time, Alice was helping a customer choose books for her grandson's birthday. We took our purchases to the back. As I placed my book on the counter, Charlie glanced up. He blinked a few times. Charlie had gorgeous blue eyes, and a charming smile when he bothered to use it. If he'd been room décor, he'd have been shabby chic.

"Ah, Lucy, very nice to see you."

"Thank you, Charlie. Nice to see you, too."

That was the extent of our scintillating conversation. He grew more animated when he rang up Vi's purchase, telling her how much she was going to enjoy her herb book and that if she took the guide with her to the botanical gardens, she'd be able to see a number of the plants mentioned in the book. He obviously knew a lot more about local weeds and herbs than about love stories.

While they shared tales of foraging for mushrooms in the Chilterns, I noticed a poster hanging on the wall, advertising the upcoming visit of celebrity author, Martin Hodgins. I was very interested to see he was doing a talk at Frogg's Books as I'd recently been involved in helping him get the credit for work that had been stolen from him more than forty years earlier. In the process I'd nearly been killed, but I'd also found a good friend in his daughter, Gemma.

Beside that was a poster asking if anyone had seen a missing Cardinal College student. Since Cardinal College was a block down on Harrington Street I took a moment to study the photograph. The student's name was Sofia Bazzano. She was a very pretty girl with long, curly brown hair. It was a casual photo that showed her with a drink in her hand and a laugh on her face. According to the poster she was twenty-one years old and last seen two days earlier. Her roommate had reported her missing when she hadn't returned home. She was a stranger to me, but I memorized her face so I could keep an eye out for her.

The mushroom conversation seemed to be winding down, so I said, "I'm very excited to see Martin Hodgins speak."

Charlie glanced at the poster and then at me. "You'd better get here early. It's going to be standing room only, I imagine. But, have you heard the news?"

"What news?"

"His publishers have announced that Martin Hodgins has a new novel in the works."

I was so delighted I clapped my hands. "I knew it. I was sure he'd kept on writing, even if only for his own pleasure all those years."

"It seems you were right."

I was about to say goodbye when I noticed another poster sitting on Charlie's desk, presumably waiting to be put up on the board. It was for an upcoming play. Cardinal College was putting on A Midsummer Night's Dream.

He followed my gaze. "You wouldn't like to post one of these in your shop, would you? Cardinal College is my old college, you see. I help out with their big production every year, my way of giving back." He shrugged. "Midsummer Night's Dream isn't the meatiest of Shakespeare's plays, perhaps, but done well it can be very amusing. Ellen Barrymore will be directing."

My eyes opened wide. "The Ellen Barrymore?"

"Yes. She teaches acting at the college. We were very lucky to get her, though, sadly this is her last year. She's going to be the artistic director of Neptune Theatre in London's West End."

Ellen Barrymore had made a name for herself on the London stage when I was a little girl. Gran had taken me to see her play Nora in Ibsen's A Doll's House back when we were studying that play in high school. However, she'd gained much wider recognition when she was cast as an alien hunter on American television in the late 1990s.

After that she seemed to make some bad choices, or perhaps there weren't any better available, in any case, her career seemed to dry up. I mostly saw her on guest spots on TV and bit parts in Indie movies.

"She's here? Working down the street?" I squealed, as excited as a fan. Which I was.

"Yes. She was a student there, twenty-five years ago now. I'll be her assistant."

"You're going to be an assistant director?" I don't know why this surprised me so much.

He seemed to be as surprised as I was. He cracked his self-effacing grin. "I won't be telling the actors what to do, or anything. My job will be to get them there on time, standing in the right spot on stage, and make sure everyone knows their lines. That sort of thing."

Alice came up, then, and rang up the grandmother's book. When the older woman left, Alice said, "I'm helping, too."

Of course she was. Anything to be near Charlie. She glanced at her watch. "It's nearly eleven. I'll get the coffee on."

He sat back down and found his place in his book. "Lovely."

She gazed at him, lovingly. I could feel how much she wanted to stroke his head. "And I made carrot cake. Your favorite."

"Yes. Excellent," he said, without looking up.

Once we were outside, Violet said, "It's an epic tragedy the way that girl pines for Charlie."

"I know. And he's so clueless. Does he even realize that she bakes him fresh cakes every day?"

"Honestly, I think you could substitute a robot with brown hair and he wouldn't notice the difference so long as he got his coffee on time."

"Poor Alice."

Vi stopped and put a hand on my arm. "Lucy, I've got the most marvelous idea." She sounded so enthusiastic that I grew nervous. "Remember how we talked about you working on your potions?"

Violet was a much more experienced witch than I and she

was always pushing me to go deeper into our craft. My problem was that my magic was powerful, but not always under my control. I preferred to stick to small spells within my comfort zone.

There was a tidying up spell that I really loved.

Actually, she'd talked about it and I'd nodded and pretended I was interested. True, she'd brewed me up a potion that healed my aches and pains, but I preferred the safety of something I could purchase at a drug store—which, since living in the UK, I'd learned to refer to as a chemist.

The idea of me cooking up something that another person might drink gave me cold shivers just thinking of everything that could go wrong.

I'd looked at some of the potions in my grimoire, good for things like curing boils and easing childbirth. It wasn't like following a recipe in a cookbook and ending up with a Cordon Bleu worthy meal. The ingredients in one of the potions included bloodroot, mugwort and nettles. I knew the resulting brew would look like sewer effluent and probably taste worse.

Vi looked altogether too excited for my liking. She said, "We're going to cook up a love potion that will make Charlie fall in love with Alice." She heaved a sigh of happiness. "You'll love it. It's like matchmaking with herbs. Brewing up a happily ever after."

With my luck, instead of cooking up eternal happiness, I'd give Alice and Charlie a case of dysentery.

CHAPTER 2

*W*e walked back into Cardinal Woolsey's and there was Detective Inspector Ian Chisholm trying to choose between forest green angora wool and a brown merino.

Meritamun, the three-thousand-year-old Egyptian witch who was my other assistant, was diplomatically agreeing with everything he said in an effort to help him choose. It wasn't working. His eyes lit up when he saw me.

"Ah, here's Lucy, now." I had a feeling he'd been putting off making a decision until I got there so he could see me.

I got a little fluttery seeing him unexpectedly. He'd kissed me right before Christmas and since then we'd been out on a few dates. We always had fun, but I think we were both wary of getting involved too fast. I, obviously, had a lot of secrets I couldn't share with a sharp-eyed detective. I was a witch, for one, and my downstairs neighbors were a nest of vampires.

He had issues of his own. Chief among them, his job. He could be called out at any time and when he was working a case he did it with a zeal and determination that I admired even as it meant he sometimes cancelled our dates at the last minute.

However, there was a warmth in his eyes when he looked at me that told its own tale. I probably had a similar expression when I returned his gaze.

He held out the two skeins of wool he was debating. "My auntie insists on knitting me another jumper. I've told her I don't need one, but she says it gives her something to do."

I completely understood how he felt. The vampire knitting club kept me supplied with new things to wear nearly every day. I couldn't turn down their gifts and hurt their feelings. I displayed and sold what I could, and wore as many of the sweaters, scarves, hats, socks and dresses as I could. I was running out of closet space.

He only had one lonely aunt to contend with. He didn't know how lucky he was. I took both the skeins he held out and replaced them in the baskets they'd come from.

Instead, I took him to the table of magazines and pulled out the newest issue from Teddy Lamont's quarterly magazine, Designer Knitting with Teddy. Teddy was a contemporary artist and knitwear designer with homes in London and LA. He'd helped bring knitting back into fashion. I'd flipped through the latest issue and seen a sweater I knew immediately would look great on Ian.

The model was featured against a Highlands backdrop, with one booted foot up on a rock. The sweater was made with variegated wool in tones ranging from navy to mulberry. It was manly and sexy. Exactly like Ian.

He looked at the magazine photo doubtfully. "You don't think it's too...Scottish?"

His name was Ian Chisholm. "Aren't you Scottish?"

"Well, my ancestors are."

"You don't have to wear it with a kilt."

"All right." He bought the magazine, which included the pattern, and the wool. "Auntie will be pleased to have a new project. Thanks."

Since I felt that he perhaps wanted a few words in private, which was impossible with both my assistants standing right beside us and listening to every word, I said I'd walk him to his car.

When we got outside, he said, "I'm glad to get you to myself for a few minutes."

Last time I'd seen him he'd suggested we get together on Friday, which, according to my calendar, was tomorrow. We walked to the end of the road where I could see his car parked. It was a Mini Cooper. Not one of the slick new ones built near Oxford, but an original model. I was certain, without even asking, that he'd disdain the redesigned ones.

"I was hoping we could see each other tomorrow night, but I've got to work late. Are you free Saturday?"

"You're working late again?" The words came out before I could stop them. I had a few issues around the 'working late' excuse. My former boyfriend Todd had said he was working late when he was working on getting naked with a co-worker. I'd caught them *in flagrante* on his kitchen table, so I wasn't the trusting soul I'd once been.

Ian was nothing like Todd the Toad and I knew he was telling the truth, but still, I experienced a flash flood of hot betrayal before I calmed myself down.

Ian misunderstood the source of my irritation. "I know I'm letting you down, and I'm sorry. It's this case." He put his purchases in his car and then turned back to me. "There's an undergrad gone missing from Cardinal. She's only twenty-one."

I nodded. "I saw the poster."

"Good. The more people looking for her the better. Her parents are flying in from Dubai tomorrow. I'll meet with them, see what I can find out, and get them up to speed on our investigation. With missing persons, time is of the essence."

"I do understand. Of course you have to do your job."

"I'll make it up to you. I'll take you for a nice dinner Saturday night. How's that?"

I thought it sounded fine and said so.

"I'll look forward to it." And then he leaned forward and kissed me. It was so casual, the kind of kiss shared by people who are a genuine couple. Was that how he saw us? Perhaps that's where he thought this was going. I had no idea and wasn't ready to ask. Ian's job would, I thought, always come first.

And I had my own issues, one of which was even now causing a cold shiver to tingle the back of my neck.

I waited until Ian had driven away before saying aloud, "What are you? A voyeur?"

"Hardly," Rafe said contemptuously, emerging from Rook Lane to walk by my side. "You put on a display for the entire street. One couldn't miss it even if one wanted to."

"Well, if you'd stop creeping around behind me, you wouldn't see what I got up to."

"I was coming to the shop to see you," he said with dignity. I completely understood that Rafe was jealous of Ian. I wished things could have been different. We were connected in some strange way, he and I, so we were always aware of each other. And I was drawn to him, but more in a moth to flame way than one that had a future.

Apart from the mortal/immortal divide, dinner dates with Rafe were always going to be awkward. He gave the raw food movement new meaning. Also, I liked to sleep at night when he was at his most energetic, and I didn't really want to get old and wrinkled while my partner remained endlessly gorgeous and looking thirty-five while having the experience, wisdom and wealth of someone who'd been around for six centuries.

None of that stopped our mutual attraction or his jealousy. Sometimes I thought longingly of my old life in Boston where I hadn't known I was a witch, when I'd worked in a cubicle and dated mortals. Okay, it had been boring and unsatisfying and the mortal I'd been dating turned out to be cheating scum, but back in those simpler days I didn't wrestle with questions like, can I be with someone who can never age or die?

It was hopeless.

And yet, when Rafe talked of leaving Oxford I panicked. Rafe was, more than anything, my friend and someone who protected me and helped me, even if he was high-handed and controlling.

"Where is he taking you tomorrow night?"

I don't know how he'd heard about my Friday night date with Ian, but Rafe tended to know way too much about my business. I turned to him and shook my head. "You really need to update your attitudes from Tudor times. No one takes me anywhere. I'm a modern woman and a feminist."

He opened the door to Cardinal Woolsey's and held it for me. After we were both inside, he didn't drop the subject as

I'd hoped. "Where are you independently meeting up with your suitor?"

Violet giggled. "He's not a suitor."

Rafe appeared baffled. "What is the correct term?"

Violet sighed and looked dreamy. "The correct term is hottie."

Rafe rolled his eyes. "I think females had more sense in Tudor times."

Now, I believed the subject would drop, but Violet had other ideas. "Where are you and Detective Hottie going tomorrow night?"

"As a matter of fact, he has to work late. We're going on Saturday. To dinner."

Rafe looked as though he were having trouble keeping his opinions to himself. Violet didn't even try. "He's working late again? And he seemed so keen on you."

Meri was watching all of us. She was trying to learn how people acted in the current age and I felt as though we weren't giving her the best role models.

"He is keen on me. But he's involved in a difficult case. Time sensitive."

"That sucks." Vi brightened up. "But we can work on our secret project."

Not so secret once Violet was involved.

Rafe didn't even ask. He simply waited. And not for long.

Violet turned to him. "Lucy needs to work on her potions so I'm helping her make a love potion."

He raised his eyebrows. "To encourage Detective Inspector Chisholm in his pursuit?"

"No!" I cried. "Honestly, Violet, I'm really not sure I want to interfere in other people's love lives."

"I can't imagine why not," Rafe said, half to himself. "You do so well with your own."

I ignored him.

Violet said, "I already spoke to Margaret Twig and she's willing to help us."

I was horrified. "When? We only talked about a love potion a few minutes ago."

She looked at me as though I were missing something obvious. "When you were outside with Ian. We don't have any time to waste. February is a very powerful month for love. Saint Valentine's Day and all that. And Margaret is the best teacher. Her love potions are famous. Besides, she's got all the ingredients and they're fresh, not like the dusty old herbs you've got upstairs."

"I don't know about this."

"Why? It's not like I'm suggesting something harmful. Poor Alice deserves love and, frankly, she'd be really good for Charlie. It's not healthy for a man to have his nose stuck in books all day."

Rafe made a noise like he was clearing his throat. Of course, as an antiquarian book expert, he also had his nose stuck in a book, or ancient manuscript or sometimes a papyrus scroll all day long.

"But maybe they aren't meant to be together. We could do more harm than good by interfering." I knew we witches had a code of honor and were never supposed to do harm. Then I presented my biggest argument. "Alice hasn't asked for a love potion."

"Only because she doesn't know we're witches." She took a step toward the door. "Shall I pop over and tell her that we're witches and we'd love to brew her up a potion to help her attain her heart's desire?"

"No." I scowled at her. Then I turned to my other assistant, who'd been a witch longer than our whole coven put together. "Meri? What do you think?"

"One must be very careful when interfering in matters of the heart," she said.

Before I could tell her how much I agreed, Rafe said, "You can ask Alice yourself what she wants. She's coming in."

I couldn't believe it, but he was right. Alice was at that very moment walking past the window of my shop. I willed her to keep walking but she slowed her steps and then turned and opened the door. The cheerful bells announced her arrival.

She looked slightly startled to find all of us staring at her. "Hello. Did I interrupt a meeting of some kind?" She took a step back. "I can come back."

"No," I said, stepping forward. "We were looking at the window display. I was wondering if I should do a Valentine's theme, though it's not a very knitting-oriented holiday."

We both gazed at the front window where I had the usual range of cheerful-looking knitted goods with all the materials to make them. I liked to fill a big basket with various colored balls of wool and, as she so often did, Nyx, my black cat and familiar, was curled up in the middle of the basket, her chin resting on a very expensive ball of silk mohair.

Alice looked lost. "I couldn't say." Even mentioning Valentine's Day made her look despondent.

Violet caught my eye and opened her own wide, an obvious hint to me to find a way to ask Alice if she wanted a love potion. I wasn't sure how I would do that without letting on that we were witches. Instead, I asked her if she was looking for knitting supplies. She'd walked into a knitting shop, it seemed like a reasonable question.

Alice blushed and spoke to the back wall. "I was thinking I might knit Charlie a sweater for his birthday."

Oh the poor woman. Violet made a sound like a moan, or that might have been Meri. Nyx gagged as though she were about to cough up a fur ball. Rafe muttered something under his breath. I ignored them all and said to Alice, "That's a nice idea. When is his birthday?" I needed to know whether we were looking for a simple pattern that she could knock off quickly or whether she had plenty of time.

Her blush deepened. "His birthday's in November. But I like to plan ahead."

I had a mental image of her sitting in her lonely flat night after night feeling connected to Charlie only because she was knitting him a sweater. I wanted to smack her and tell her to stop acting like his mother. But how could I?

I glanced at Rafe and made a sideways motion with my head. He nodded slightly and took the hint. With a brief word of farewell he headed out the front door. Now there were only the three of us witches in the shop and Alice, who was planning to knit a sweater for a man who already treated her like a comfy cardigan he'd wrap around himself when he was chilly. No one had romantic feelings for an old woolen sweater.

I barely needed Violet's prodding. I was filled with compassion for this lovesick woman and wanted to help her. "Do you really think Charlie's suddenly going to notice you because you knit him a sweater?"

I knew it was brutal to let her know that I was perfectly

aware of her hopeless infatuation. However, I wanted to help her and I couldn't until she'd asked me. If she wanted a love potion, I would do my best to make her a good one. But, until I knew that she wanted our interference, I wasn't prepared to step in.

Alice's head jerked up at my words and she stared at me. "You know?" she asked in mingled horror and relief.

I nodded. "I've seen the way you look at him."

Her shoulders slumped, and she picked up a ball of pink cashmere and began to knead it in her hands like stubborn bread dough. "I didn't think anyone knew. Of course, I'm being silly. He doesn't notice me. Every night I go home and I tell myself he doesn't care. But then, I'll think of a moment when he smiled at me, and I'll remember how happy he looks when he's eating my cake. And I think, maybe, one day he'll realize that I'm the best thing that's ever happened to him."

"How long have you been working at Frogg's Books?"

She looked even more defeated. "Nearly three years."

"I'm not great at math, but that's nearly a thousand cakes you've baked him. Probably twice that many cups of tea and coffee you've made him. Has he ever shown any romantic interest in you at all?"

She was stroking the ball of wool in her hands now, the way I sometimes stroked Nyx when I needed comfort. "Once, he asked what I was doing on Saturday night. I remember to this day the way my heart started to pound and I thought he'd finally realized how I felt and perhaps reciprocated my affection." She shook her head. "But all he wanted was for me to come in and help him do a Saturday night stock-taking."

"Ouch," Violet said. She drilled me with her gaze. I didn't need mental telepathy to know she was encouraging me to explore the idea of a love potion with Alice. I nodded and drew in a breath.

"Alice, what if you tried a new approach?"

She looked thoughtful. "I've considered baking cookies instead of cake. Or maybe I should bring in chocolates. They do say the way to a man's heart is through his stomach."

I wasn't exactly a femme fatale, but any fool could see that Alice's attempts to get Charlie to notice her weren't working. "Not food. I think, after three years, you have proven that doesn't work."

"But what does work?" Her eyes were filled with appeal. "I'm willing to try anything."

Violet flipped her hair over her shoulder so the bright pink stripe she'd dyed in her black hair fluttered like a ribbon. "Are you sure he's worth it? Any man who can't work out from a thousand freshly-baked cakes that a woman's in love with him sounds a bit thick to me."

Alice fired up in her beloved's defense. "Charlie's not thick. He's one of the most intelligent men I know. He gradu- ated with a degree in English literature from Cardinal College here in Oxford and he got a distinction. He's read every significant novel that you could name. He's read some things in Latin and once I saw him reading a book that I think was Greek."

Violet made a rude sound. "That's book learning intelli- gence. I'm talking about emotional intelligence. I'd say your Charlie has the emotional intelligence of a small rock."

Alice pondered her words, then wrinkled her nose. "Maybe a medium-sized rock."

I had to tread carefully in suggesting a love potion. Maybe they hadn't burned witches in a very long time, but I wasn't taking any chances. "I've heard about a woman who lives out in the countryside. She claims she can make a love potion. I've never tried it, and I don't know if it would work, but I wonder if it's worth a try?"

Alice looked at me as though I might be insane. "A love potion? What is she, a witch?" Her voice went high on the last word as though she felt foolish even mentioning creatures that didn't exist outside of horror novels and children's fairy-tales. Hah, little did she know.

Violet and I exchanged a glance. "You could refer to her as a wise woman," Vi said.

I thought Alice would immediately dismiss the idea. In fact, I hoped she would and then Violet would leave me alone and not expect me to concoct a witch's brew. However, after thinking about it for a minute, Alice shrugged. "What do I have to lose? Nothing I've tried so far has worked." She laughed and her whole face lightened. "Why not? If the potion doesn't work, I'll be no further behind."

She looked at each of us in turn and I thought, if Charlie ever saw this sweet, mischievous expression on her face, he might get his nose out of his book for five minutes and take notice of this remarkable woman who was pining for him.

Before I had a chance to say anything, Violet jumped in. "That's excellent. Lucy and I both know this woman, we'll get her started on your potion right away."

Right away sounded much too soon for my liking. Alice also looked uncertain. "Do I have to meet this wit-woman?"

"No, no," Violet said hurriedly. "She's very reclusive."

Alice looked relieved that she didn't have to visit a witch. I didn't blame her. I wished I didn't have to visit Margaret Twig either. I hadn't forgotten the time she stole my cat. Fortunately, Nyx was a very resourceful familiar and she'd managed to get herself out of Margaret Twig's clutches without any help from me. However, I knew that with Margaret there was always a price to be paid.

Almost as though she'd read my thoughts, Alice said, "Is this potion very expensive?"

"I think twenty-five pounds should do it," Violet said.

Alice laughed again. "I spend more than that each week on cake ingredients." She opened her bag and counted out the money in cash.

I began to feel suffocated as the reality of what we were about to do closed in on me. "Are you sure about this?" I asked her.

She put her hands in the air in a helpless fashion. "Every year I send him a Valentine's card anonymously. And every year he doesn't know who his secret admirer is. I don't even disguise my handwriting. Maybe this year I'll at least get his attention."

That sounded more like a desperation plan than a sensible one but I kept my mouth shut since I could see how enthusiastic Violet was about the idea. She picked up the money and folded it carefully and put it in her handbag. She got very efficient then. "There are a couple of other ingredients you'll need to bring us."

I had no idea what she was doing, but of course, she'd made love potions before. She counted out the items on her fingers. "First, I'll need a strand of hair from each of you, also, some fresh blood, yours as well as his, and photographs of you both. If you're pictured together that's even better."

Alice's eyes widened. "Fresh blood? How am I to get Charlie's blood? I want him to fall in love with me, not end up in the hospital."

"Don't be such a drama queen. He works with books and paper all day, doesn't he ever get paper cuts?"

"Not very often."

Violet leaned closer to Alice. "You'll have to be resource-ful. Perhaps a small accident with the scissors, or the sharp knives you open boxes with. It doesn't have to be a great deal of blood, but she will need some."

I waited, hopefully, for Alice to demand her money back. Instead, she said, "How do I transport this blood? Assuming I'm able to get it."

"If you soak up a little of his blood on a cotton handker-chief, that will do." She shook a warning finger at Alice. "No tissues, mind. The blood must be on proper cotton or linen."

For a second she seemed to waver in her resolve. I didn't blame her. Stabbing someone in order to get them to fall in love with you didn't exactly scream romance. But, she was desperate enough that she agreed. "When do you need it?"

"Saturday, after our shops close." Then she looked at me, obviously remembering that I had a date on Saturday night. "No, wait, tomorrow. As soon as you have the blood, the hair, and the pictures, you can pop them down and leave the lot with one of us."

Alice drew in a shaky breath. "I'll do it."

Then she put down the somewhat mangled ball of pink wool and, with a hurried thanks, left.

As soon as the door shut behind her I turned on Violet. "Tomorrow? We're doing this thing tomorrow? With no time to prepare?"

"Really, Lucy. Don't you keep up with your lunar calendar?" She pointed out the window, "Tomorrow there will be a full moon."

Of all times for Ian to cancel a date, did it have to be during a full moon?

My only hope was that Alice would be too squeamish to draw blood from the man she loved.

CHAPTER 3

*L*ater that afternoon, I heard the unmistakable sounds of one of the vampires coming up through the trap-door from their underground lair and into my back room. I had particularly acute hearing, better than either of my two witch assistants, so I wasn't worried that the two customers currently shopping in my store would be alarmed.

Unless it was my grandmother sleepwalking again. We'd nearly cured her of the habit, but it was quite alarming when a sleepwalking vampire, who'd been well-known in the neighborhood and had once owned this shop, wandered in looking sleepy and confused. Just in case Gran was up to her old tricks, I slipped behind the curtain and into my back room. To my relief, it wasn't my undead grandmother, but Theodore, a former policeman, coming up through the trap door, which led to the tunnels below my shop where some of the vampires lived.

Theodore had a round, babyish face and pale blue eyes. Those eyes were currently brimming with anticipation. Since the biggest problem the vampires had was boredom, I was always pleased when they had a project, so long as it was something harmless that didn't involve me. He said in a whisper, "All clear out front?"

I shook my head and put a finger to my lips. I heard the two ladies say goodbye and then peeked out to make sure they were gone. In a normal voice I asked, "What is it?"

"They've asked me to paint the sets for A Midsummer Night's Dream. I'm very excited by the possibilities, the whimsy, the magic, the enchanted wood."

Theodore had done a lot of scene painting for amateur theater productions over the years. Since he'd only recently moved to Oxford, he could still go out in public without raising eyebrows. The vampires tended to move location every generation or so in order to avoid suspicion since they remained eternally whatever age they had been when they were turned. Rafe, I knew, was past the time when he should have left, but Theodore hadn't been in Oxford more than about five years, so he had lots of time left.

"That's wonderful," I said. I wasn't entirely certain why he'd come up here, was it just to tell me the good news?

He looked bashful. "I'm glad you think so, Lucy. I wondered if you'd like to help me."

I wasn't sure I'd heard him correctly. "You want me to help you paint the sets? Theodore, I have absolutely no artistic talent whatsoever."

He looked even more bashful. "You don't need talent, just be willing to wield a paintbrush. I'm very shy around young people, especially the ladies. I wondered if you could come with me on Saturday. It's the initial meeting of the full cast and crew. If you could come with me, just until I get comfortable."

A bashful vampire? Now I'd heard everything. But, as I'd grown to know the undead knitters who lived beneath the shop, I'd become very fond of them. Theodore had knitted me some particularly beautiful sweaters and one shawl that I really loved. I wanted to help him. Plus, I thought it might be fun to help behind the scenes of a play. Maybe I'd get to spend time with Ellen Barrymore.

Since Charlie and Alice would both be there, I'd have a chance to see if the love potion had any effect. So, after making sure that both Meri and Violet thought they could do without me on Saturday afternoon, I agreed to help Theodore.

I HALF HOPED that Alice would lose her nerve, especially in the blood-drawing department, but she hurried in about three o'clock on Friday afternoon, looking terribly guilty and somewhat pale. She held a canvas bag in trembling hands and, waiting until there was no one in the shop, rushed forward and said, "I did it. It was horrible, but I did it."

Violet beamed at her, "That's wonderful, Alice. How did you get the blood?"

"I stabbed him with a knife." She looked so shaky I thought she might faint.

Violet's bright smile dimmed. "You did what?"

She waved a hand about and I saw that there was a large sticking plaster on her index finger. "Don't make me feel worse than I do. I couldn't think how I might get blood from him, and so, instead of cutting a slice of cake in the kitchen, like I usually do, I brought the cake out to the desk. I'd brought in my sharpest paring knife from home. I asked him to hold the plate.

"He barely paid any attention. He put his hand on the plate and still kept reading his book. So, it was easily done, though it took a great deal of courage and resolution. I sliced his thumb and pretended I thought it was the cake."

She looked so horrified I had to suppress a laugh. "What did he do?"

"He jumped right out of his seat and shouted a word that I didn't even believe he knew."

"Oh dear. Did it bleed very badly?"

"It was all right once I'd tied the handkerchief quite tightly around the wound. Of course, then I was in a pickle because I needed that handkerchief. He kept waving me away when I offered him a sticking plaster but, finally, I prevailed. The handkerchief is in the bag, along with mine. The hair's in there, too, and the picture."

"You did very well," Violet said, peeking in the bag. Her eyes widened. "Blimey, you're sure he's still alive?"

"Please don't make jokes. It was very stressful." She looked near tears.

"Why don't you come in the back," I said. "I'll make you a nice cup of tea."

"Thank you," she said with real gratitude. "I can't remember the last time someone made *me* a cup of tea."

I smiled. "Sorry I don't have any nice cake, but I do have some homemade gingersnaps."

She shuddered. "I had to throw my cake away. It's got blood all over it."

I shuddered myself.

Then, she looked at the tin of biscuits. "Your grandmother

always used to make gingersnaps."

In fact, she'd made this batch but I didn't let on. "Yes, I know. She left me the recipe and, whenever I make them, I always think of her."

While the kettle heated, she said, "Lucy, do you know this person?"

I didn't want to admit intimacy with Margaret Twig so I said, "I've met her."

"And you think she's good?"

I thought of some of the spells I'd seen her cast. "Oh, she's very good."

She sighed. Her hair was in a neat braid that had flipped to the front and she began to play with the end of it. "You read in Victorian novels about heroines who pine away for love, and do the most ridiculous things for their beloved and I always thought I was too sensible for that." She accepted a cup of tea with thanks. "And then I met Charlie. In my sane moments I think it's absurd to attempt a love potion, but I am that pining heroine. I'll try anything to have Charlie. Anything at all."

"I understand. I can't promise the potion will make Charlie fall in love with you, but for twenty-five quid I suppose it's worth the gamble."

She nodded and swallowed. "When will the potion be ready?"

"I'm not positive, but I think now Violet has the ingredients, she can take them to the wise woman and brew it up right away. I think you might have it by tomorrow."

A dreamy look came over her. "Perhaps by this Valentine's Day, I will have my heart's desire."

"I hope so." Then I opened the tin. "Have a biscuit."

CHAPTER 4

*M*argaret Twig looked far too pleased to see us. I sensed her triumph that she and her kind were drawing me deeper and deeper into the craft.

She was wearing one of her long, drapey garments. Not quite dress, or shawl or cloak, but some combination of all of them. This one was of dark green velvet with gold threads running through it. I thought fleetingly that the costumers of the Midsummer Night's Dream production should borrow it.

There was always something theatrical about Margaret Twig and I was certain she'd dressed for the potion making. Under the cloakish garment she wore black trousers and a black silk chemise and a string of fat purple beads around her neck.

Her hair was its usual wild tangle of gray-white corkscrew curls and her bright blue cat's eyes were uptilted in anticipation. Even her red lipstick looked freshly applied to her thin, smiling lips.

Since Violet had warned me to dress appropriately, I'd also made an effort. I wore a midnight blue sweater-dress that

Sylvia had knitted. I'd wanted to wear it with the pretty diamond necklace she'd given me, but after Margaret had demanded my cat in payment for the last favor she'd done me, I didn't want to tempt her with diamonds. Instead, I wore a necklace of rose quartz. I'd had Meri put a protection spell on it for me.

Margaret's eyes immediately went to the necklace and her small white teeth gleamed in amusement. "Really, Lucy. Where's the trust?"

Violet glanced at me sideways with an I-told-you-so expression. She was wearing a mulberry colored sweater that she'd knitted herself. With the rainbow stripe she'd dyed down the front of her long, black hair, it was quite a striking combination. Under that she wore black tights and black half boots.

As Margaret beckoned us to enter, I caught the scents of cinnamon, some kind of citrus, and a darker note I couldn't identify—something between bitter chocolate and mushroom.

"Come in, come in." She walked ahead of us, her heels tapping on the flagstone flooring. Margaret's cottage was made of the honey-colored Cotswold stone and had to be three or four hundred years old. It was the sort of cottage that appears on postcards of the Cotswolds, with its thatched roof, climbing roses, and the soft, green fields surrounding it. For, like the witch's house in fairy tales, Margaret's cottage was all by itself in the remnants of the ancient forest of Wychwood.

When the house was first built, I imagined the trees would have been thick all around it, but now it was mostly fields. Still, the place was isolated. I suspected Margaret had a powerful spell surrounding her cottage, discouraging builders or developers from taking an interest in the nearby land, or perhaps I was giving her too much credit and she was on some kind of land reserve.

As we grew nearer to her large kitchen, I felt my stomach tighten with nerves. As though she sensed my uneasiness, which, no doubt, she did, Margaret said, "It's very exciting, brewing your first magic potion. It's natural to be apprehensive. But, when you see the results of your efforts, you'll be enthusiastic to continue the practice."

All I cared about was not poisoning anyone. *First, do no harm*, I repeated the phrase in my head like a mantra.

When we walked into the kitchen, the scents I'd picked up earlier were masked by the smell of beeswax candles. She had them burning all around the huge stone hearth.

Margaret had a fire lit under a black, cast iron cauldron. She had several sizes and this was the smallest, though it probably held a gallon of liquid when full.

I thought she could have put a pot on the stove just as easily, but preferred the drama of using a cauldron over open fire.

There was liquid already in the pot, bubbling away. I grew increasingly apprehensive. "I thought I was making this spell." At least, I wanted to know what was going into this potion before I handed it to an unsuspecting human.

"You are, my dear. There's nothing in there but distilled water. I thought I'd get the pot on to save time."

Did I believe her? I lifted my gaze to hers and read the challenge in her blue eyes. If I threw out the contents of the pot and started again, I'd lose her goodwill, whatever there was of it. Besides, what possible reason would she have to sabotage the love potion? I decided to trust her. Sort of. "Thank you."

"You've brought the blood and hair and so on?"

Violet lifted the canvas bag. She nodded and reached for it. "Excellent."

"And here's the twenty-five pounds," Violet said, counting out the money.

Margaret sniffed. "You can't put a price on love." I noticed she took the money, all the same.

"Right. Have you got a recipe or do you want to use mine?"

Violet and I had discussed this. I'd found what I thought was a love potion in our family grimoire, but the writing was old and faded and splashes of liquid, presumably love potion in progress, had made a few of the words indecipherable. I explained that I'd brought the spell book along, anyway, hoping that our family recipe and Margaret's were similar enough that we could fill in the blanks.

She looked amused, but then she usually looked amused whenever I spoke.

"Right, then. Let's get started." She held out her hands and we three joined together in the candlelight. She said a few words, clearing us of negative energy and thoughts and focusing on joining our power under the full moon.

When we were done, she said, "All right, then, let's see this spell of yours." I brought out the ancient book of spells and carefully opened it to the love potion. Margaret read over my shoulder. Nodded, muttered, "Milk thistle and rose hips. Interesting. Otherwise, it's much the same. Yours is, perhaps, a little heavier on the honeycomb and coriander while mine adds a few more pansies."

Margaret then opened her own grimoire and we compared recipes. In the end, we decided to go with Margaret's recipe since it was more recent and tried and true, but I was pleased to be able to fill in some of the blanks in my own recipe. Not that I imagined I'd be using it very often, but I'd rather have my own potion than have to come back to Margaret Twig's house.

Margaret's herbs and other ingredients were all either grown in her extensive gardens or foraged locally, so I trusted them more than the bags and bottles in Gran's kitchen that had grown dusty and pale.

It was surprisingly fun adding a pinch of this and a sprinkle of that and watching the bubbling liquid gleam in the candlelight. When we had the basic potion done, Margaret directed me to take the two bloodstained handkerchiefs from the bag as well as the other items. Alice, being an orderly sort, had put a few long, curling hairs from her own head into an envelope and sealed and labeled it. I didn't know where she had collected the much shorter hairs from Charlie, but I could imagine her lovingly pulling stray hairs from his sweater, or the collar of his coat.

The photos were in a separate envelope. Both looked to be snaps she had taken on her phone and had printed. Charlie, as usual, reading behind the desk, no doubt unaware his photograph was being taken and she'd taken a selfie. Being particularly anxious that this spell should work, she had also included a picture of the two of them together. This looked as though it had been taken at a reading with a famous author. She was standing beside Charlie, but his head was turned away from her toward the person who had been cut out of the photograph. All that remained of the author was a bit of their shoulder and arm.

Margaret told me to drop the two handkerchiefs into the bubbling brew along with the hairs. I hoped somebody was going to strain this potion before anyone drank it. I stirred the liquid with a heavy wooden spoon and after a few minutes she told me to lift the two handkerchiefs out. Presumably, by this time, enough of the blood had come off the fabric to do its job.

The handkerchiefs certainly came out looking clean. If the brew failed as the love potion, it might work as a stain remover.

Under Margaret's direction I then waved the pictures through the steam while reciting the following verse.

One sip of this brew the trick will do
To open the beloved's eyes
Full to yearning and to sighs
Pricked with Cupid's arrow be
So I say, so mote it be

On the last phrase, the brew suddenly boiled quite furiously. I glanced at Margaret, worried I'd done something wrong, but she nodded in approval. "Yes," she said, with another of her secretive smiles. "I believe you will find that most efficacious."

I felt a qualm of doubt. "She only wants him to ask her out."

Margaret shook her head at me. "This isn't like one of those chain coffee shops where you can order your drink exactly the way you want it. Magic is never an exact science. That's why we call it magic."

I glanced between the two other witches who didn't seem

to share my fears. "It can't do any harm, can it?"

Margaret laughed, a soft, husky sound. And then quoted, "The course of true love never did run smooth."

Strange that she should quote from A Midsummer Night's Dream. I wondered if she knew I'd be at the first rehearsal tomorrow.

We poured the brew into a clear glass bottle and Margaret stuffed a cork into the opening. Not content with that, she then melted some red wax to seal the top.

I knew that Alice would be using that potion in the next day or two. "Was it necessary to seal the bottle?"

Margaret looked at me and shook her head, her eyes twinkling wickedly. "Adds to the mystery. The punters like to get what they paid for."

It seemed to me that half of Margaret's magic was pizzazz and showmanship. Still, she was more powerful than I so I kept my mouth shut.

As Violet and I gathered our things together and prepared to leave the warm kitchen, Margaret put a hand on my arm. "I keep forgetting you're a novice. Don't forget, once the potion's been drunk, the effects will only last for three days. Make sure the lovers are together when they drink. That will make it more powerful."

I felt slightly better knowing that the love potion would wear off.

When we left Margaret's cottage and got into Violet's car for the drive back to Oxford, she said, "I can't wait to see what happens. This is so exciting."

I replied noncommittally but really, I thought I could wait a very long time before having strangers drink a love potion that I had brewed. Perhaps, forever.

CHAPTER 5

The first full meeting for the cast and crew of Cardinal College's upcoming production of A Midsummer Night's Dream was held that Saturday afternoon. I knew that Violet was disappointed not to be able to come along, but, first of all she wasn't part of the cast and crew, and second I needed her to run the shop. Meri was doing better every day but she was still easily thrown.

I wasn't completely heartless, though. I let Violet come with me when I went to give Alice our potion.

We walked up the street to Frogg's Books. The day was mild for February and pale sun glinted off the puddles after a recent rain. I was so nervous I felt sick, but Violet chatted with excitement as we made the short walk to the bookstore. "Do you think she'll feed it to him while we're there?"

Before I could answer, she said, "I so want to see it. I bet it will be like the final scene in a romantic comedy when the hero looks at the heroine and you know he finally gets it, he's totally in love with her and you know they will live happily ever after and have fifteen children."

"I wouldn't wish fifteen children on anyone," I said.

She giggled. "You know what I mean. True love."

I stopped her in the street and she turned to look at me in surprise. "What if it's not true love? What if Charlie really doesn't want Alice? Who are we to interfere with his heart, his desires?"

She sent me a rather superior smirk that I think she learned from Margaret Twig. "All it will do is create strong infatuation. You know how when you have a crush, and you're really keen on someone, you can't think about anything else but that person? But then it passes. And it either turns into true love or it fizzles out. All we're doing is creating the same feelings of a little crush. The rest is up to Alice and Charlie."

"And it's really only going to last three days?"

She nodded. "It's really only going to last three days. If she slips him the potion today, he'll either be back to his clueless self by Tuesday or they'll be in love. It's like relationship kindling. There will be a nice blaze but if the big logs on the fire don't catch then that bright blaze will burn out quickly."

By this time, we'd reached the door of Frogg's Books. Violet laughed at me. "Stop looking as though you're doing a terrible thing. You're trying to help two people fall in love. What could be better than that? Now, put on a happy, confident face and let's get that kindling burning."

I doubted I had much of a happy face on but she was right. There was no point looking as though I brought bad news with me. We walked in and, as usual, Charlie had his nose buried in a book. Alice was tidying bookshelves and an older woman was dusting which suggested that she was employee rather than customer.

Alice glanced up when the door opened and her face went bright red and then deathly pale. She dropped the book she was currently shelving so it smacked as it hit the ground. Charlie glanced up. He saw Violet and I and greeted us and then went back to his book. Alice meanwhile got to her knees and picked up the dropped novel and shelved it completely crookedly with shaking fingers.

When she was back on her feet, she hurried towards us and motioned us outside. She had no coat on but didn't seem to notice the cold. She walked us past the window so Charlie couldn't see us from inside. "I don't know if I can do this. I was awake most of the night worrying. What if I trick him into falling in love with me when he never really wanted me? Wouldn't that make me a terrible person?"

I was glad I wasn't the only one who had these moral qualms. Violet immediately launched into the crush and the kindling story after which Alice looked much calmer. "So it will only last three days? And, if he's not in love with me by Tuesday then I can move on with my life."

I applauded her good sense. "Exactly."

She put a hand to her heart. "I've wanted this so badly and for so long. Now I'm frightened."

Violet took her hands and spoke soothingly. "Alice, you are a wonderful woman. Charlie would be lucky to have someone like you. All we're doing is helping him see what's under his nose. The rest is up to him."

She shook her head. "I just have this awful feeling that something's going to go wrong."

Well, that made two of us.

Violet opened the same canvas bag that Alice had brought her offerings in. She showed her the potion and explained that she should put a few drops into any kind of liquid. "It will have a distinctive flavor, so you should put it into tea or coffee or wine or something that has a strong flavor of its own."

She nodded, her fingers pleating and unpleating the cloth bag that contained the potion.

"Try and slip it to him so that he'll look at you right after he drinks it and that will deepen his infatuation."

She laughed slightly hysterically. "That's not difficult. We're together nearly all the time." She seemed to think. "Though, getting him to look at me rather than the pages of his book might be more difficult. Maybe if I stamped a few pages of David Copperfield on myself and lay down on his desk, that might work."

Violet and I exchanged a glance. Surely she was joking. With Alice it was difficult to tell. She seemed to think about it, further. "I know, I'll put the potion in a thermos of coffee and take it up to the theatrical meeting this afternoon. He won't be able to read a book then, he'll have to look at me."

"Excellent idea," Violet said with enthusiasm. "Getting away from that bookshop is probably a good idea, too. An unfamiliar setting could make him see you in a new light. Oh, this is so exciting. I wish I was going to be there."

Alice looked quite panicked. "I wish you were, too."

Violet said, "Don't worry, Lucy will be there. She's helping with the scene painting."

Alice looked relieved. "I'll feel so much better, Lucy, knowing that you are there."

Violet and I walked back to Cardinal Woolsey's and the feeling of dread didn't go away. But, I comforted myself with the notion that the potion would wear off by Tuesday. How much could go wrong in three days?

THEODORE'S EYES lit up when he came up into my back room ready to walk up to the cast and crew meeting.

"Why, Lucy, you are wearing the sweater I knitted you. I am pleased with it. It brings out the blue in your eyes."

I laughed. "I don't know about that, but the sweater is exquisite and if anyone asks I will tell them to come to Cardinal Woolsey's where we have a simpler version of this pattern and the very same wool. I never pass up a marketing opportunity. I hear from some students who shop here that knitting is very relaxing, especially if they're stuck in long, boring lectures."

I'd also chosen this particular sweater to give Theodore confidence. I wanted my bashful vampire to feel that his artistic endeavors were appreciated.

He had a sketchbook with him and I saw that he'd made some initial rough drawings. He'd drawn a magical wood with winged fairies. Another scene showed a vaguely Greek looking manor house. "These are lovely," I said.

"There will be a lot of tree painting, I'm afraid. So much of it takes place in the magic wood. Mabel and Clara are both keen to help with the painting, too. They like to keep busy."

I was a firm believer that a vampire who was busy with arts and crafts was less likely to cause trouble. And, since the local vampires mostly lived under my shop, I was happy to do anything I could to prevent trouble.

I'd never been inside Cardinal College before, so I was happy to have an opportunity to get beyond the gates. Theodore and I stopped at the Porter's Lodge and gave our names and our reason for entering college grounds. Once we'd been admitted, we crossed the quad, which, in better weather, would be bursting with flowers, its fountain giving a backdrop of pleasant splashing noises to visitors and students on their way in and out of the college. Now, it had the desolate feel of a garden in winter. Even the ivy covering the walls looked chilly.

Theodore said, "The gardens behind the college are much more interesting. An early arborist had every variety of tree planted that would grow in this climate. Many of those trees are hundreds of years old. It's quite lovely when the weather's nice."

Theodore gallantly opened the main door for me and I walked inside Cardinal College. I don't know what I'd expected, something along the lines of a castle perhaps, but the hallway that met my eyes was a combination of a stately home and my high school back in Boston.

There was rich, dark wood paneling on the walls, the ceilings were high and dotted with plaster roses, but there were also modern notice boards with bits of paper stuck to them. Part-time jobs available, reminders about scholarship applications and, sadly, a poster of that missing girl. I wondered how Ian had made out with her parents last night. I hoped they'd find her soon.

As I followed Theodore down the hall, I noticed that it smelled like a school. Like young bodies and, obscurely, a bit like onions.

I understood why I had smelled onions when we passed a

dining room with a series of very long tables. At the far end raised up on a sort of stage was the head table.

As we passed on I could hear the banging pots that suggested we were passing the kitchen. The smell of onions grew stronger.

We walked all the way to the end of the corridor and out another set of doors and across yet another quadrangle to a more modern-looking building. Maybe something from the 1920s or 30s. The sign on the door announced that this was the theater wing. The minute we stepped inside I heard the buzz of conversation and somewhere a loud laugh.

"I love the first day, it's so exciting," Theodore said. If he hadn't been a vampire, his cheeks would've pinkened. As it was, his tone of voice gave away his excitement.

I felt kind of excited too. Even though I was only the assistant to the scenery painter I wished I had brought my own notebook. I felt like it was the first day of school and I longed for freshly sharpened pencils and a new lunchbox.

We got to the theater itself and I was impressed with its size. There was seating for several hundred people in front of a large stage. A female student with a clipboard stopped us at the entrance and when we gave our names directed us through another door. "The first meeting is in the big rehearsal hall," she said. "Write your names on a name tag, that way everyone can sort out who everyone else is."

I wrote *Lucy* with a purple sharpie pen on the nametag. It was one of those stick-on labels that either didn't stick on properly or ruined clothes. I wasn't going to glue the label to my pretty sweater, so I stuck the nametag on the collar of the white blouse I was wearing beneath. Theodore wore a gray T-shirt under a black blazer, so it was a simple matter for him to stick his label in the middle of his chest on top of the cotton T-shirt. He chose a black sharpie and wrote *Theodore: Set Painting*. I didn't want to be known as the set painting assistant so I left the single word: Lucy. If anyone wanted to know what I was doing here they could ask.

We walked into the large rehearsal room and I imagined this was how a lone bee might feel flying in to a very big, busy hive. There was nothing but buzzing and movement and a sense of hierarchy being worked out which, I suspected, involved some stinging.

I took a moment to simply take in the scene. There were probably fifty people present. It was immediately obvious which ones were the actors—they strutted about looking important, while the crew seemed to search nametags looking for people they knew.

I must admit, I also searched for a familiar face. It didn't take me too long to spot Charlie and Alice. Alice was staring at Charlie with longing, as usual, but she looked quite perturbed. I understood why. She had hoped to feed him the potion here, when he didn't have his nose in a book, but she hadn't counted on the man's obsession with the written word. Any written word.

He had found a script and was sitting back in a chair, one leg crossed over the other, his reading glasses perched on his nose and the script open in front of him. We could have been on the Titanic going down, with alarms shrieking and pandemonium on deck, and I doubt he would have noticed.

CHAPTER 6

*P*oor Alice. She clearly didn't know what to do. She needed him to drink some potion and look at her, not a book. He was already in love with books. He didn't need any extra help there.

No doubt she'd wait until they were back at the shop and slip the potion into his tea, then find an excuse to get him to look up at her.

I decided to take a walk around the room and find out who these people were. I'd never taken part in a theatrical production before, so it was kind of fun. We weren't here to change the world or debate politics, the entire point of this play was to entertain. No doubt the students involved would earn some kind of college credit, but it seemed to me they were more excited about playing dress-up while being the center of attention.

There were four of them in particular who caught my eye. Perhaps because they were all young, gorgeous, and confident. No one got into Cardinal College who wasn't bright, so I imagined they were highly intelligent as well. They seemed to be acting out a plot as complicated as anything Shakespeare ever came up with. There were two women and two men. One of the women wore her red-brown hair in a stylish, short cut that emphasized her big brown eyes and a wide smile with teeth so white they reminded me of Hollywood. She was tall and shapely and she used those eyes, her smile and her swaying figure like grappling hooks to draw in her prey. The two men seemed to be enjoying the game, as much, I thought, in competition with each other as genuinely wanting that girl. The second woman wasn't so flamboyant. She had strawberry blonde hair pulled back in a messy bun, fair skin with freckles and red cheeks as though she spent a lot of time outdoors.

The young men were just as gorgeous and as well-aware of their appeal as the girl with the short hair. One wore a Cardinal College sweatshirt over designer jeans and boots that probably cost more than my entire wardrobe. He was dark with that careless I-just-got-out-of-bed hair and an I-could-eat-you-all-up grin. The other wore a plain white T-shirt and a navy blue sports jacket over jeans so molded to his body they left little to the imagination. He was as fair as the other was dark and his eyes seemed only half open. He needed a shave but his whole attitude suggested he couldn't be bothered.

I couldn't hear the conversation but had a strong sense that these four were at the top of the food chain. While I was watching, the dark-haired man turned and headed in my direction. Maybe I didn't avert my gaze quickly enough, because he walked right up to me. Well, swaggered might be a better term for the way he moved. He stopped in front of me and lifted a careless finger to the collar of my shirt. "Lucy," he read. "And what's your place in all of this? You're not a student, are you? I'd have noticed."

I bit back a smile. He was probably three or four years younger than I, but did he really think his heavy-handed come-on was working? "I'm a volunteer from the community. I'll be helping with the sets."

He nodded. "I'm Miles Thompson. I'll be playing Lysander. You'll design an extra special set for me, won't you?"

I ignored the nonsense about building sets to make him look good. "Congratulations. You got one of the leads."

He chuckled. "Our illustrious director chose this play to fit the talents of her acting troupe. It's a play all about mismatched lovers and confusion. And we know all about that." He suddenly looked very cynical and world-weary for one so young.

"Are those the other leads?" I pointed to the three still talking together.

"That they are." He pointed to the group. "Scarlett Baker reckons she will be the next Keira Knightley. She's playing fair Hermia, naturally. That's Jeremy Booth, he's playing Demetrius." He pointed to the blonde. "And that's Polly. She's playing Helena." He watched her. "She's a bit intense."

I didn't want to abandon Theodore, so I looked about for him.

While my attention wandered, so did Miles Thompson's and he excused himself to go and talk to a very pretty redhead. There was a long table with a big catering sized urn of coffee, hot water for tea, and a tray of not very interesting looking biscuits. I noticed Alice hovering around the coffee urn and suspected I knew what she was about. I wandered over in time to see her pour coffee into one of the white ceramic mugs provided. She added milk and sugar and then with a sidelong glance at Charlie, she slipped a silver flask from her bag.

No doubt she thought the glass beaker was a bit peculiar looking, or she was afraid it would break. At least, if Charlie saw her pour something from a flask she could say it was a bit of brandy to warm him up.

I thought she hesitated and then her shoulders straightened and she gave one firm nod before tipping a little of the potion into the coffee mug. I watched her walk over to Charlie, who glanced up and accepted the coffee with a preoccupied smile.

A newly-familiar voice said, "A little tipple for our first meeting. Excellent idea." Before I could stop Miles Thompson, he'd grasped the flask which Alice had foolishly left sitting out beside the coffee urn and took a swig.

"No, wait," I said, but it was too late.

As he swallowed, his face twisted as though he'd sipped drain cleaner. He made a gagging motion. "That is without doubt the worst swill I have ever tasted."

I stood in horror not knowing what to do as his equally posh friend who was to play Demetrius came up and said, "What's this? Your private vintage?"

With a wink at me, Miles said, "Yeah. Help yourself."

I reached out, desperate to get the flask, but Jeremy laughed and turned his back saying, "Your turn next." And he too took a sip. Like his friend he grimaced and gagged. "My God that's awful." He glared at Miles. "Did you bring this?"

He shook his head. "No. It was that girl over there." And he indicated Alice.

Unaware that her potion had fallen into the wrong hands, Alice was still fussing over Charlie trying to get him to take a sip of his coffee. I rushed over to her. "Alice, you've got to get your flask back. Those boys have it."

She glanced back at me and then followed my gaze to where Miles and Jeremy were walking around with her potion. Her hands flew to her mouth. "Oh no. What do I do?"

I had no idea. I'd never been in a situation like this before. I said, "You'd better get it back. And quickly."

"But Charlie might drink the potion and look at someone else."

"That can't be helped. Anyway, he's back to reading the script. I think he's forgotten his coffee. Leave it while you sort out the flask."

She went rushing off and I'd have gone to help her except I glanced up and saw Detective Inspector Ian Chisholm walk through the doorway. If he had tracked me down here to tell me he couldn't make our date tonight, I was going to be seriously unhappy. But, when he saw me, his face lit up. It was clear he hadn't known I would be here.

I walked forward and said, "Ian. Are you helping out with A Midsummer Night's Dream?"

He shook his head. "Fraid not. I'm here on official business."

Ian glanced around the room and I thought he'd found the person he'd come in search of. But, before he could take a step forward, a kind of quiver went through the room. I glanced up and there, on the stage, was Ellen Barrymore. In person.

"I can't believe I'll be in the same room with Ellen Barrymore," I said softly to Ian. I'm a fangirl.

The director clapped her hands and said in a powerful voice, "Welcome, everyone. Please find a seat and we'll begin."

Everyone shuffled around into chairs. I saw Alice arguing with the two young men who seemed like they were having great sport in keeping the flask out of her reach.

I turned to Charlie to see if at least he'd taken a sip of his doctored coffee, and yet a new horror met my eyes. Scarlett Baker, the very pretty young actor who was to play Hermia, walked up to Charlie. She said something that made him look up. I wasn't completely sure how that potion worked but I thought it would be best if Alice was the first person Charlie set eyes on after he had sipped that coffee, not the all-too-attractive Scarlett.

"Excuse me," I said to Ian, already moving to head off the latest disaster.

Ian said, "Don't mind me. I'll get myself a cup of coffee and hang about in the back until your meeting is over." I nodded, barely paying any attention to him as I was so anxious to get between Charlie and Scarlett. I waved to get Alice's attention but she was pleading with the boys to return her potion.

One horror at a time. I headed toward Charlie and Scarlett in time to hear the young woman say, "Lovely. Coffee. I haven't had any today." Before my horrified gaze, she lifted his mug to her mouth and took the most provocative sip of coffee I have ever seen any person take.

"No!" I shrieked. They both turned to stare at me. I scrambled for a reason as to why I had cried out. Several people nearby had stopped to stare at me. Including Polly who walked over to Scarlett as though to protect her.

I said, "It's flu season. We shouldn't be sharing cups or we'll spread germs." I sounded more motherly than Alice, and Charlie, obviously rather flattered at Scarlett's attention, grinned. For a guy who spent so much of his time with his nose stuck in a book he was awfully attractive when he looked up and smiled at a woman.

He said, giving Scarlett a sideways glance and Polly a wink, "I'll take my chances with a germ or two." He took the mug from her hands and, very deliberately, put his mouth where hers had been and took a sip.

Weirdly, she didn't pay any attention to him. Scarlett was staring at me as though we were long-lost sisters who'd just reunited. She stepped forward and pushed her hair behind her ear with a nervous hand. "I don't think we've been introduced?"

"I'm Lucy. I'm helping with set painting."

She drew in a quick breath. "I do hope you can help me." She ran her hands down the side of her very trim figure. "You see, I'm so tall. I want to be certain that you design the sets in the magical forest so they don't make me look like I'm one of the trees."

I had something else to think about but these actors' vanity, what with Alice scampering around after that flask and all the people who seemed to be drinking that potion. I wished it *was* alcohol in that flask. I'd have taken a big hit myself.

Once more, the director called for everyone to take their seats. I'd had enough of the two actors teasing Alice over that potion. She needed to get over to Charlie and quickly. The two actors were all over her, teasing and flattering her, but she was almost tearful in her pleas for them to give her back her flask. I was about to tell them both off when the blond one, Jeremy, looking very sheepish passed her the flask.

It was empty.

CHAPTER 7

S he let out a shriek. "What happened to the p—the drink that was in there?"

Oh please, please let them have spilled the potion all over the floor. Instead, they fell to giggling. "Share and share alike," Miles said and snorted and pointed. I followed his gaze to the coffee urn. Oh, no. They couldn't have.

I looked at all the people currently drinking coffee and wondered how many of them had filled their cups after those wretched fools had tipped the rest of the potion into the coffee urn. To my horror, I saw Ian sip out of a mug. He was looking at Scarlett, his eyes obviously drawn by her vivacity and quick movements.

She seemed to be looking for someone and then she saw the group of us, Miles and Jeremy, beside Alice and me. She came over with her quick step but instead of sitting beside the boys, she took the empty seat beside me. She leaned closer. "Lucy, I must get your mobile number."

She was really serious about this set business. I explained that I was only an assistant painter but she shook her head and pushed her phone at me. With a helpless shrug I put my mobile number into her phone and then immediately my phone buzzed.

She said, "I sent you a text so you'd have my number, too." She gazed at me anxiously. "You will call me?"

I was about to tell Scarlett that she should talk to Theodore, but at that moment Ellen Barrymore got up on stage and clapped her hands. She stood very still for a moment and her very stillness captured all the attention in the room. Ellen Barrymore was forty-four years old. I knew this because I had done an Internet search on her before I came. I felt a little flutter of excitement just being in her presence.

She was a classic beauty who wore her dark brown hair long and very straight. She was wearing a red woolen dress that was somehow both commanding and sexy. With that she wore black stockings and black pumps. A long gold chain hung from her neck and chunky gold earrings flashed at her ears. She looked every inch the diva.

Hush fell immediately over the cast and crew and we sat, waiting. Ellen Barrymore was known for her intelligent acting, her graceful walk, but most of all for her voice. It was low-pitched and slightly husky. We were treated to it now. "Thank you all very much for coming out today. Some of you are students, here to gain acting experience and school credit, and some of you are volunteers from the community. I want to personally thank each and every one of you for your commitment. The parts are already cast and the actors and understudies will remain here with me."

Chairs began to scrape and papers to rustle.

"Stage hands, builders, set designers and painters and

costumers will each be directed to your rooms by the lady in the back with the clipboard. She is Alex Blumstein and she will be indispensable to all of you, as she is to me."

There was a slight creaking and shuffling noise as most of us turned to look at the woman standing in back. She didn't look as though she wanted to be indispensable to anyone. She looked as though her feet were in shoes a size or two too small. She was on the short side and stocky and she held her clipboard as though she might bash you over the head with it as soon as write something on it.

Beside me, Scarlett leaned closer. "She's an absolute dragon. Don't get on the wrong side of Alex Blumstein whatever you do."

I whispered back, "Thanks for the tip."

The director went on, "As this will be my last season and my last play with the college, I am determined that this will be our best production yet." She smiled her glorious smile at us. "I have my professional pride after all. Fortunately, I am aided by some of the best talent I have ever worked with. And, as many of you know, I have worked with the best."

She paused for the appreciative laughter that ran through the room. "I predict that within a decade some of you will become household names and celebrities. And every one of us today will be a part of that success, whether we stitched a costume, helped create the magical forest through lighting and sets, or simply made coffee."

At the word *coffee* I felt my insides shudder.

"And so, as we like to say in the business, let's go break a leg."

I could have listened to that wonderful voice forever, but everyone in the room was clapping and some of the students who knew her were whistling and cat-calling. I joined in the applause, hoping that the potion I had had a hand in creating didn't make trouble right at the beginning of this production. I felt as guilty as though I had shouted out "Macbeth" to a bunch of superstitious actors.

I was sad to hear that Ellen Barrymore was leaving. I had enjoyed a momentary fantasy where she might discover a passion for knitting and drop by my shop from time to time. I liked the idea of even working on the same street as someone whose talent I admired so much. I turned to Scarlett, "Is Ellen Barrymore really leaving?"

"Oh yes. We're all devastated. Well, not too devastated, because she's going to be the artistic director of the Neptune Theatre in London. We're all hoping that she will hire us." She glanced around and then dropped her voice to a whisper. "Naturally, she can't say anything, but she's let Miles and Jeremy and me know that she'll keep an eye out for places for us."

"That's fantastic," I said. I didn't know much about the acting business but everyone talked about lucky breaks and it seemed to me that these gorgeous young people were about to get theirs. Not that nature hadn't already given them plenty of lucky breaks. Simply being bright and well educated enough to get into Oxford was a huge break, but to also be beautiful and theatrically talented seemed like an extra heaping of good luck.

I pictured myself one day telling my friends how I had painted the green on a tree in front of which the famous actors Miles Thompson, Jeremy Booth and Scarlett Baker had performed. It was as close to fame as I was likely to get.

"Well, good luck on the first day. I'd better find out from the dragon lady where I'm supposed to go."

As I looked around for Theodore I noticed he was with a student in jeans and a hoodie who seemed to be hanging on his every word. She looked as though she were meeting her idol. Then I noticed the coffee cup in her hands. Oh, dear. She motioned a friend over and the three of them began looking through Theodore's sketch book.

I stood up and nearly bumped into Ian, who'd come right up to us. But he wasn't looking at me, his attention was on Scarlett.

"Excuse me," he said. "I'm Detective Inspector Ian Chisholm. I wonder if I might ask you a few questions?" When Scarlett looked at him his cheeks and neck went a ruddy color. I hoped he wasn't coming down with something.

Scarlett looked quite pleased. "A detective inspector? How exciting. How can I help you?"

His color darkened and I realized the man was blushing. He cleared his throat and pulled out the same picture I'd seen on the missing person's poster at the bookshop. He asked, "Do you know this woman?"

Scarlett glanced at the photograph. "Of course I do. She's Sofia. I take a drama class with her. I'm sorry to say she's not very good." She shrugged theatrically. "I suppose one shouldn't really say that when the poor girl's missing. Have they found her yet?"

Ian shook his head. "We know she spent some time here on the day she disappeared."

"At the college? Well, of course, this is where she goes to school."

"No. Here, in the theater wing the day before yesterday. Did you see her?"

Scarlett wrinkled her nose. "We were all in and out that day. Ellen had posted the parts so I imagine everyone who auditioned popped in. I don't think Sofia got chosen for anything much." Then she gasped. "You don't think that's linked to her disappearance do you? Could she have been so distraught that she—" Then she shook her head. "No. That's ridiculous. Sofia wouldn't—"

"But you didn't actually see her that day?"

"No. I don't think so."

He pulled out another photo, this one looked to be a printout from a CCTV camera. It showed a guy who looked like a student, cute with dark shaggy hair and a slightly disreputable air about him. "What about this man? Do you know him?"

She only glanced at the photo and then nodded. "Of course, I do. That's Will." She glanced around. "He should be around here, somewhere."

"Does Will have a surname?"

"Course he does. William Matthews. He's playing one of the rustics."

"Was Sofia seeing him, do you know?"

"No, I don't know. Ellen doesn't like her actors dating, says it messes with the production, so anyone who's involved with somebody else in the group keeps it secret."

He gave her one of his business cards. "Well, if you think of anything, anything at all that might help, please don't hesitate to call me. Any time."

She glanced at the card and back at Ian. "Try Miles."

Ian kept his gaze steady on her face. "Who's Miles?"

"The one over there who's completely in love with himself."

We both looked over. The two who'd been larking with the flask stood together. One dark, one fair, both looked to be in love with themselves. Scarlett obviously realized she had to be more specific. "The dark one."

"And why would he know?"

She let out a breath. "I think he and Sofia were friends. *Are* friends. I think she fancied him."

"I thought you all kept your romantic feelings secret?"

She lifted a shoulder. "As I told you, Sofia isn't much of an actress. You could see it in the way she looked at Miles, touched him when she thought no one was looking."

A guy about my own age strode toward us. He had to be an actor. He had dark, wavy hair that any woman would kill for because it fell in such perfect waves away from his face. He was rather pale, with intense green eyes and a slightly scruffy beard.

Tall and thin, he vibrated with energy. I bet he could eat anything he wanted and never gain an ounce. He wore disreputable looking jeans, a red flannel shirt that looked as though he'd slept in it and he carried a small backpack over one shoulder.

I thought he was the one from the CCTV photo Ian had just showed us. He glanced at me and Ian and then said to Scarlett, "I've just arrived, what did I miss?"

She rose and went towards him. "Darling Will. Hopelessly late as usual."

They double cheek kissed, French style, and Will said, "Darling Scarlett, hopelessly gorgeous as usual."

She took his hand and turned him towards us. "This is

William Matthews. He's the one in your photo. Will is playing Snug the Joiner. Though he'd really hoped to play Lysander."

Will might dress casually and show up late as though he didn't have a care in the world but his jaw set hard at her words and I thought he had really wanted that part. Perhaps his showing up late and slovenly was a kind of protest.

Ian, meanwhile, looked at him keenly. He asked, "You're William Matthews?"

Will nodded. "That's right. Who's asking?"

Scarlett said, "Oh, it's terribly exciting. This is the police. They're asking about Sofia. She's still missing."

Will swallowed. "The police?"

"Yes. Detective Inspector Ian Chisholm." This time he gave his name in a way that sounded almost like a threat. "Do you know Sofia Bazzano?"

"Of course. We all do. She's one of the actors."

"When did you last see her?" Ian didn't mention the photo. He wanted to see if Will would entrap himself.

Will looked very much as though he wished he hadn't arrived quite so soon. "I saw Sofia the day before yesterday."

"The day she disappeared."

"Yes. I suppose so."

"Where did you see her?"

Will slipped his backpack off his shoulder and placed it on one of the chairs, which gave him a chance to turn away from Ian's questioning gaze. When he turned back he said, "Here. We'd all come in throughout the afternoon to find out what parts we'd been given in the play. I bumped into her."

Ian waited. In fact, we all waited. Finally, Will said, "She was upset. She didn't get the part she wanted. Well, neither did I." He hesitated and then said, "I took her down to the pub and bought her a pint."

I found I'd been holding my breath and when Will admitted he'd been in the pub with Sofia I felt my lungs begin to work again. That was likely where the CCTV photo had come from.

"Anything else?" Ian's words were hard and sharp edged.

"No. Look, we're friends. She'd been crying and I wanted to make her feel better, that's all."

"And did you? Make her feel better?" Wow, Ian could do bad cop when he wanted to.

Will shook his head. "Honestly, I don't think so. Ellen had been pretty brutal with her, apparently told her she'd never make it as an actor. Sofia was pretty cut up. I stayed for about an hour and then I had to leave. I offered to take her home but she said she wanted to stay for another pint. So I left."

"And with all the posters that are plastered over the campus, you didn't think to phone and tell us that? Do you know that you are likely the last person who saw Sofia before she disappeared?"

Will looked hot and very uncomfortable. "I didn't think. I mean, there were other people at the pub. I couldn't possibly be the last person who saw her."

"Did she mention going away? Have a trip planned? Do you have any idea what may have happened to her or where she's gone?"

"No. Obviously, if I did I'd have rung up. She talked about giving up but I thought she meant acting. In fact, I'm sure she did. Look. I left her in the pub and she was fine. I can't tell you any more."

"What time did you leave the pub?"

"I don't know. About six, I think."

"And where did you go?"

He scratched his lightly bearded cheek as though it itched. "I went back to my room to study."

"Can anyone vouch for you? A roommate?"

He shook his head. "I don't have a roommate. I don't think anyone saw me."

Ellen, the director, clapped her hands. "Everybody in scene one please bring your scripts and come on up to the stage." She looked down at the people who were still left and was clearly puzzled by the fact that there were two of us in the group who were obviously not her actors. And, in that lovely, carrying voice she asked, "Can I help you?"

Ian introduced himself once more and asked if he could have a minute of her time.

She looked as though she might argue and then, with a slight shake of her head, climbed down the stairs at the side of the stage and came over to us. She was just as lovely when she grew closer, though her age was beginning to show in the slight crinkling around her eyes and the laugh lines around her mouth. She held out her hand to Ian and introduced herself. "How may I help you?"

Unlike me, Ian didn't seem star-struck. He held up the photograph of Sofia Bazzano, explained that he was investigating her disappearance and asked if Ellen Barrymore knew the girl. She barely glanced at the photograph.

"Yes, of course I do. Sofia is one of my actors. A lovely young woman with a bright future."

"When did you last see her?"

"The day before yesterday. I'd posted the full cast list, you see. All of them were in and out to find out what parts they'd been assigned."

"Did you speak to her?"

"Yes, I did. She came to my office to see me." Scarlett and Will were both listening and no doubt anyone close enough to hear anything was avidly eavesdropping. "Sofia didn't get the part she was hoping for. She came to ask me why." Ellen smiled, sadly. "It's the most difficult part of my job to give out rejections. So many lovely, talented actors come through this program. Of course, all of them hope to be the next Kenneth Branagh or Kate Winslet. I assigned Sofia rather a small part when she'd auditioned to play one of the main lovers."

She looked up at the stage where, already, actors were settling themselves, getting ready.

"I told her, as kindly as I could, that she might want to think about other options for a career. Perhaps it sounds cruel, but she struck me as a sensitive girl and I would rather she were let down gently, while still at school, than suffer the brutal rejections that will await her in the real world."

Ian said, "Will here said she was crying when he bumped into her."

"Oh. I am sorry. She seemed perfectly composed when she left my office." She glanced at Will and smiled at him fondly. "I hope you cheered her up?"

He glanced at Ian before answering. "I took her to the pub."

She reached out and touched his shoulder. "That was kind of you." She turned back to Ian and said, "I do hope you find her soon. As I said, she's a lovely girl." Then she turned. "Will, do stay. I've put you in as the understudy for Demetrius. If Jeremy breaks his leg, you'll stand in for him."

He nodded but didn't look thrilled. No doubt he'd hoped to play the part, not remain in the wings hoping Jeremy Booth had an accident.

Ian handed Ellen Barrymore his card. "If you see or hear from Sofia, you will let me know."

"Of course. I'm certain she'll show up. She's a Hero, not an Ophelia." And she laughed softly. "Forgive me, I tend to think of people as Shakespearean types. Hero is a sweet young innocent in Much Ado About Nothing while Ophelia tragically loses her mind and takes her own life in Hamlet."

She looked at Ian as though waiting for him to thank her and let her get back to her duties but he said, "Interesting that you should choose Hero. She hides away and pretends to be dead after her heart is broken."

Her soft laugh was as musical as her speaking voice. "I'm impressed. The police officer who knows his Shakespeare. I wasn't making any connection between Sofia's disappearance and Hero's actions, merely suggesting that both are highly romantic and somewhat naïve."

He said, "Thank you for your time. I'll let you get on."

The actors gathered around Ellen Barrymore. I leaned closer to Ian. "Isn't she remarkable?" I asked softly.

"Yes." He wasn't looking at Ellen, though, he was looking at the group containing Scarlett and Polly.

"I'm going to go and catch up with the set design and building group."

I thought he'd walk out with me but he said, "All right. Think I'll stay here and watch for a bit."

"All right. See you tonight."

"Mmm."

As I was heading back to Alex Blumstein to find out

where to go, Scarlett came running up and stopped me. "Lucy, wait. I was thinking maybe you could work with the actors, help us run lines and so on."

"Oh, but I'm supposed to help with sets."

She rolled her eyes. "Really, you'll be painting rocks and trees and things. Much more interesting to work with us." She leaned in, "Shall I ask Ellen?"

Of course I'd rather work with the actors than paint scenery, and then I'd be able to spend time in the presence of Ellen Barrymore, but I'd come here to support Theodore. "I'll have to check. If my friend doesn't need me and Ellen approves, then, of course."

"Excellent, then it's settled." And she ran back.

Theodore found he had more scene painting helpers than he needed, what with the two women who'd suddenly volunteered to help him after drinking the magic-laced coffee, and Mabel and Clara who'd promised to help, so I went back to the main rehearsal room to help.

I watched them, this excited group of actors, with a world-renowned director, at their first rehearsal. It would have been an entirely happy moment if Ian wasn't sitting, watching, a reminder that one of the players was missing.

CHAPTER 8

When I got back from the rehearsal, I wanted nothing more than to kick back with a cup of coffee and relax. Instead, I found Meri looking excited and agitated. It was half an hour before closing time and I worried she'd had an awkward encounter with a customer.

"Is everything all right?" I asked. And where was Violet? She was supposed to keep an eye on Meri in case anything came up that she didn't understand. Like electricity.

"Oh, yes." She put her hands together as though I were her queen and she was my slave. She hadn't done that for months, so she was clearly emotional.

"Meri, what is it?"

Before she could answer, the door opened and Pete walked in. Pete was an Australian, an archaeology grad student who also happened to be a wizard. "G'day, Lucy. You're looking good."

"Pete!" I held out my arms and he pulled me into a robust hug that nearly cracked a rib or two. Pete had helped me defeat the soul-sucking demon who'd tried to destroy me and all my kind. At the time, I'd thought he was sweet on me, but the minute he met Meri, he was smitten.

I thought she felt the same. He was working with my archaeologist parents at a dig site in Egypt and when my mom and dad had suggested Meri come for a visit to her homeland, she'd seemed really interested. Of course, we couldn't let her get on a plane by herself. There was too much that could go wrong for a woman who hadn't really been active in three millennia. Pete had volunteered to come to England and escort her back.

I felt suddenly sad, knowing that now Pete had arrived, I'd be losing Meri, who'd become a friend as well as a shop assistant. He read my feelings with ease. "I'm sorry I can't stay very long, but I've got to get back. I've booked a flight back tomorrow."

"So soon?"

"Fraid so. We need to get some critical funding and your dad thinks Meri could be a big help in identifying some household items we don't recognize."

She looked at me with her eyes shining. "Lucy, I could be really useful to your family. After all you have done for me, I wish to try."

"Of course, you do. And you'll be going home."

She nodded. "Yes. Though I do not think I shall recognize very much."

"Not a lot changes in the desert," Pete said. "You'll recognize that. And I think the bugs will be familiar."

We laughed. Then Vi came in from the door to my flat. "Oh, good. You're back. I was helping Meri pack. I lent her one of your suitcases. Hope that's okay."

"Of course." I didn't have any travel plans. And my parents would return my case next time they came to visit.

We closed the shop and then Violet said she had to go. She had a date with a guy she'd met online. Pete said he wanted to take Meri out on the town. He invited me to come along, but I was happy to say I also had a date, so they could spend an evening alone, renewing their acquaintance.

I was happy for Meri, but once again, I was looking for more help in the store. I dreaded going up to the corner grocer and putting up yet another notice for a new assistant.

Tonight, I wouldn't worry about the future. I'd enjoy my evening out with Ian. Who knew where it might lead?

I GOT ready with extra care for my date that night with Ian. He'd hinted that we were going somewhere special for dinner and so I dressed for the part.

Having spent so much of the day with actors today, I understood the power of costume. I had a little black dress I'd splurged on in the January sales. I wore it with the diamond necklace Sylvia had bought me and low-heeled pumps. I wasn't sure about a coat and so popped down to ask Sylvia, who had an eye for fashion and always knew the latest trends.

Popping down to see Sylvia involved going to Cardinal Woolsey's, into the back room, opening the trap door and climbing down a set of stairs that led to a tunnel that ran beneath my shop. It was dark and smelled musty but I'd been down here so often that I barely thought about it. I tripped along the stone path until I came to the ancient oak door and knocked.

It was my good luck that Sylvia herself answered the door, gorgeous in a black silk floor-length negligee. Her silver-white hair was sexily tousled. She'd obviously just woken up. I apologized for coming so early but she waved me inside. I explained about the date and my coat issue.

She nodded approvingly when she saw the dress. "Very nice. You're dressing like a woman for a change."

"How do I usually dress?"

She wrinkled her nose. "A cross between a Harvard co-ed and a middle-aged housewife." She dropped her voice. "It's all those hand-knitted jumpers you insist on wearing."

My jaw dropped. That was so unfair. "How can I avoid wearing sweaters when you all keep making them for me?"

She shrugged elegantly. Sylvia did everything elegantly. "You don't have to wear them all."

But I did. I was too nice to reject the gifts that came my way from the vampire knitters. Once I'd worn the sumptuous knitted silk sweater in midnight blue that Sylvia knit, or the complex work of art that Theodore made me, how could I refuse to put on the sweater Mabel so lovingly crafted, even if it did make me look like a giant tea cozy? Before I could argue my point, she asked, "And what are you doing with your hair?"

"My hair?" I touched the blonde mass that curled past my shoulders. I'd washed and blow dried it. What more did she expect?

She shook her head. "Come," she ordered. I came. We went into her private suite of rooms and into the large bedroom. On the walls were stills from her heyday, when she'd been a movie star. There she was across from Douglas Fairbanks, and in another, enjoying cocktails with Greta Garbo. Her bedroom was like something out of a twenties film, with blue and silver bed linens and sleek art deco furniture.

The lamplight was soft. If it weren't for the lack of windows or any kind of natural light, we could have been in a five star hotel room.

She sat me before a dressing table with triple mirrors, though the mirrored surfaces were covered in photographs. It must be difficult for someone so vain to manage without ever seeing her own reflection, but I suspected that she and my grandmother helped each other with hair and makeup. She plugged in a fancy curling iron and, while it was warming, brought out her cosmetics case. I'd only planned to do my usual beauty routine—slick of mascara, a bit of eyeliner to be fancy, and the rose lipstick I wore when going out, but Sylvia had other ideas.

Before I could protest, I was being expertly made up. I thought about arguing and decided that with a vampire as strong-willed as Sylvia it was easier to let her make up my face and then wash off the cosmetics when I got back upstairs.

It was surprisingly soothing being pampered and beautified after the hectic day. I tried not to think about the potential love tangles caused by the potion I'd helped make. I consoled myself that Margaret Twig had said the effects would only last for three days.

How much could happen in three days?

"Close your eyes," Sylvia commanded.

I did and felt a brush slide across my lids, then something that felt bristly and a cool slickness on my upper eyelid.

"And look up." When I did, she slicked on mascara, not once but twice.

She stepped back, holding my chin in her hand and surveyed her handiwork. She looked as serious as a painter contemplating her masterpiece. "It's a great shame you don't do more with those pretty blue eyes. Of course, they'll never rival mine. In my prime a Maharajah presented me with a set of perfect sapphires which he said were the precise color of my eyes." She smiled in reminiscence. "I contemplated marrying him, but becoming a Maharani meant I'd have to give up the theater, and I couldn't make such a sacrifice. Not even for him."

"What happened to the sapphires?" I was certain if she had such jewels Sylvia would wear them. She wasn't one to hide her light, or her diamonds, under a bushel.

Her full lips turned down at the corners. "The financial crash happened. The 1930s happened. I sold them. I'd have bought them back but they're in a private collection now." She shrugged. "One day I'll buy them back. I have plenty of time."

She busied herself with the curling iron. Since I had no idea what she was doing, I tried to be philosophical. I had more than an hour until Ian was picking me up. I could redo my hair as well as my makeup in a pinch. Sylvia had been in the theatrical world and I imagined she still kept up, though from a distance.

I asked her, "Do you know Ellen Barrymore?"

She narrowed her eyes slightly as though trying to remember who that was. "Oh, yes. Know of her. She was quite good, one of those pretty young things that seemed to have a future. But she fizzled out. Most of those young girls do. Not many of them have the staying power of The Dames." She said it with reverence, and I knew she referred to Helen Mirren, Judi Dench and Maggie Smith. "I heard she went into teaching."

"She did. In fact, she's directing A Midsummer Night's Dream at Cardinal College."

"Ah, that's why Theodore's going around looking so pleased with himself."

"Yes. He's painting the sets and I'm helping him."

"Good for you."

"I have to be honest. I was a bit starstruck. I mean, she's so famous."

"She's a teacher." She leaned in, always one to enjoy a gossip. "Also, she's not a real Barrymore, no relation to Lionel, Ethel or John. I suspect she took that as a stage name, hoping it would make her seem like theatrical royalty."

"Well, she's moving out of teaching. Next year she'll be the artistic director of the Neptune Theater in London." I was pleased to be able to tell her something she didn't know.

Sylvia tugged the curling iron free and stepped back. Nodded, pleased with her work and came at me again. "That was clever of her. Yes, clever indeed."

"What do you mean?" I knew so little about the world of London theater.

"I imagine she used her time at Oxford to pave her way back. She's directed a few plays and if she's very lucky, one or even two of her pupils will make it big. Perhaps, under her direction. Yes, very clever. She'll never be a star again, but she's hoping to shine in the reflected brightness of a new star."

"That's rather cynical."

She chuckled. "Welcome to show business, my dear. You'll learn all about human nature at its worst working in the theater." She chuckled again. "What fun."

When she was done, she stepped back and her face softened. "Lovely. You were right to come down. I'm always happy to do your hair and makeup."

"Thank you. But I really came down to ask about a coat."

"Of course. I have just the thing."

And so I found myself going back upstairs wearing an evening coat that had no doubt taken a turn on the fashion runway in Milan not so long ago. I fervently hoped that Ian didn't know anything about fashion, for I had no way to explain the expensive coat.

Sylvia called Gran in to see me in all my glory before my date and Gran clasped her hands to her bosom when she saw me. "Lucy, you're so pretty tonight. Your young man will be proposing before you know it."

I laughed. "I'm not too worried about a proposal. I just hope he doesn't get caught up in a case. He takes his work very seriously." I air kissed both women, so as to preserve my face and then went back upstairs, through the dark shop and up again to my flat.

I headed straight to a mirror and, while it would be too much to say I didn't recognize myself, I definitely enjoyed a Cinderella moment. I wouldn't go out like this every day, but I wasn't going to wash away Sylvia's efforts, either.

The woman staring back at me looked sophisticated and definitely womanly. Sylvia had used silver and gray on my eyes, done something with my skin that made it glow, and the deep pink lipstick definitely made me look like a woman hoping to be kissed.

Which was a good thing.

My hair looked glamorous but not overdone. In fact, it was perfect. I looked like me, but a more polished, grown-up version of me.

I couldn't wait to see Ian's expression when he saw me.

He was picking me up at seven and, since he was usually punctual, I was ready a couple of minutes before. Seven came and went and by seven-fifteen, I started checking my phone for missed calls or texts.

Nothing.

By seven-thirty I was irked. I called and got voicemail. "Hi, Ian, It's Lucy." *Great start. He's a detective. He knows his name, and yours.* "I'm wondering if we got our wires crossed. Was I supposed to meet you somewhere? I thought you were picking me up. Anyway, give me a call."

I hung up, then texted him.

Ten minutes later he called, sounding harassed. "Lucy, so sorry. Something's come up. I can't stop. I'll call you tomorrow." And then he was gone.

CHAPTER 9

Something's come up? That was his big excuse? I sat there, feeling foolish and then annoyed. Sure, I understood that he was a busy cop but he'd promised me and if he was going to cancel, couldn't he have done it before I got fancied up?

I was far too dolled up to sit home alone on a Saturday night. I had my pride. If Ian was too busy to take me out, I'd go out with a friend.

Trouble was, I didn't have many friends in Oxford. Gemma was back in London. Meri was out with Pete.

Violet was on a date. In fact, everyone seemed to be on a date but me.

I was contemplating walking down to the local pub on my own when my phone rang again. I hoped it was Ian with an explanation, or at least a better apology, but it was Scarlett calling.

I was going to leave it, then thought perhaps she'd like to go to the pub with me. She'd seemed keen to be friends and, right now, I could use a friend.

"Hello?"

"Lucy, I'm so glad you're there. It's Scarlett." Her voice was pitched low.

"I know. I'm glad you called." I could hear the noise of people laughing and talking in the background and thought she was probably already at the pub.

"Look, I need to you to do me a favor."

I was not in the mood for favors. "I was just going—"

"That detective from today asked me for dinner. I don't know why I said yes. I think I was hungry, and he is sort of sexy, but he's brought me to this fancy place and he keeps trying to hold my hand."

I felt as though a bee had got stuck in my ear. I heard buzzing. I shook my head. "The detective from today asked you out?"

"Yes. He's got that dopey puppy look they get when they're obsessed with you. I can't stand it. Can you ring me in five and say you're having an emergency? I'll tell him I have to leave."

"Tell him you have to leave," I repeated faintly.

She dropped her voice. "Then maybe you and I can do something together."

Her words were clear and perfectly audible, she was used to projecting to the back of a theater after all, but I couldn't make sense of them. "Wait. Back up. Who asked you for a date? Who are you having dinner with?"

"I told you. The detective from today. Ian something or other."

"Detective Inspector Ian Chisholm?"

"There's no need to shout. I can hear you fine. Yes, that's him."

"And he's taken you to a fancy restaurant? And he's got the dopey lovesick puppy look?" I needed to be absolutely certain.

"Yes. You've got to help me."

I smiled. Grimly. "I'll be glad to rescue you from that annoying dopey puppy. Delighted, in fact."

If I hadn't been seething with a combination of hurt, anger and disbelief, I might have wondered why she didn't call one of her actual friends. Why was she calling me?

But I was in no state to think clearly. Instead, I waited the five minutes and then I called Scarlett. I said I was Polly and that I'd just broken up with my boyfriend and I was distraught. Scarlett did the rest. I asked her where she was and when she mentioned the restaurant I nearly wept. I'd have loved a romantic dinner there.

I had enough sense to leave the designer coat behind. Instead, I slipped on my regular wool coat over my dress. I grabbed the car keys and got into Gran's old Ford. Then I drove to the restaurant. It was a couple of miles out of town. I'd read about it in a magazine. It had a Michelin star, or maybe two. It could have a whole firmament full of stars and I wouldn't be eating there anytime soon.

When I pulled up out front of what must once have been a stately home, Scarlett was waiting, looking impatient. Ian was with her. Even as I drove toward them I could see that he was pleading with her. The guy who could barely manage to peel himself away from his desk for me had stood me up to make a fool of himself over a college student.

I pulled up beside them and leaned over and opened the door. Brilliant detective that he was, Ian didn't even notice. I could hear him. "Scarlett, please, tell me what I've done. I'll fix it. I only want to be with you."

Oh, magic words to my ears. "Get in, Scarlett," I all but snarled.

Ian glanced at me then, seeming irritated at the interruption. Then he saw me and his eyes widened. "Lucy. What are you doing here?"

"I might ask you the same question." I said. I wished Sylvia could see me. No actress could have delivered the line with more withering scorn. Ian looked guilty and confused and, Scarlett was right, like a lovesick puppy.

She got into the car and slammed the passenger door shut.

I peeled away so fast gravel shot up. Ian took a few jogging steps after us. "Scarlett, Lucy, wait."

I slowed down enough to open my window. He jogged closer and I stuck my hand out the window and flipped him the bird.

CHAPTER 10

"Thank you for rescuing me," Scarlett said as soon as we'd pulled onto the road leading back to Oxford. I accepted that she was a drama student and so inclined to turn everyday events into high tragedy, but she'd been on a date with the man who'd rejected me to be with her. If anyone should be acting out, it was me.

I wasn't in the mood for drama, however. I was too mad. And a bit guilty. *It was the potion.* Of course it was the potion but I couldn't believe a previous commitment didn't override the effects of water and a few herbs.

Anyway, if he was going to fall in love instantly with anyone, shouldn't it have been Alice? That was her blood and hair he'd been drinking. Why choose Scarlett?

Not her fault, I reminded myself as the actress stretched out her long legs in the cramped passenger seat and looked over at me, a smile in her eyes. "Where shall we go?"

No wonder men fell for her like bowling pins. She really was beautiful. "Do you have any ideas?"

She put her head back against the headrest. "What about a quiet night in?"

I appreciated that Scarlett had experienced a stressful day and evening, but I'd spent more than an hour being made up and primped. And I was wearing heels. I was going out if I had to go alone. "I thought maybe we'd go to a pub," I said. "I'm wearing a dress."

She chuckled, looking at me closely. "Of course you are. And you look amazing. We can go to The Bear Inn. Some of the theater crowd will be there. It will be crowded, but fun."

"Perfect." And when Sylvia asked me if I'd enjoyed my evening, I could lie and say it had been fantastic. With luck she wouldn't pry and find out I'd been stood up by my date. It was a faint hope, but at least if I could tell her I'd gone to a pub I wouldn't sound quite so pathetic.

Would I?

The pub had a fun atmosphere, was full of students, and Detective Inspector Ian Chisholm was very unlikely to turn up here. I might be a little overdressed but frankly I didn't care. Better to be overdressed and out somewhere than sitting home watching television with my cat.

Naturally, Scarlett knew a number of the people there. Miles and Jeremy were standing with Will and Polly and several other people who had been at the meeting earlier and presumably were helping in some way with the production. When he saw me, Jeremy Booth looked behind me as though searching for someone. Then he asked, "Did your friend Alice come with you?"

When I said she wasn't with us, Jeremy and Miles both began vying for Scarlett's attention. If I'd thought this through I'd have suggested we go somewhere where neither of us was known. It wasn't that I resented Scarlett getting so much male attention, but I felt raw and vulnerable. I knew it was the potion making Ian act crazy, and there was an ironic justice in me being punished this way for messing with people's love lives but still, I had my female vanity, and it was hurting.

Sitting in the corner watching yet more men ignore me in favor of Scarlett did not sound like the best way to spend my Saturday night. However, even as Miles and Jeremy both made room for Scarlett to sit beside them, she was waving them away. "There's room for two here, Lucy," she said, pushing a humorous looking guy down a hard bench to make more room. She settled me beside him and then said, "What can I get you?"

I was about to protest that she didn't have to buy me a drink when she said, "No, never mind, I know exactly what you want." She walked rapidly toward the bar and I think every single one of us at the table watched her go with various expressions ranging from blind infatuation to jealousy and, in my case, worry about what she was going to bring me to drink.

She returned with two sparkling drinks. When I raised my eyebrows she said, "Champagne cocktails. I think they suit the occasion, don't you?" I didn't normally drink champagne cocktails, but then I didn't normally get stood up, either. Perhaps she was right and this was exactly what I needed. I'd parked the car back home and we'd walked over, so I wasn't worried about drinking and driving. We clinked glasses and settled side-by-side.

The evening wasn't a roaring success, at least not for me, but I tried to act like I was having a good time. Scarlett turned out to be much nicer than I had believed her to be. She ignored the guys and spent all her time talking to me, telling me funny stories about school and asking me all about myself.

The guy she'd made move turned out to be called Liam and he was playing Puck in Dream. Liam tried to hit on me but Scarlett glared at him. "Can't you see we're having a discussion here?" She asked him, opening her eyes wide. To my amusement, he muttered an apology and moved to sit beside a girl I think was named Lucinda who was working on costumes.

About eleven I felt the cool chill down the back of my neck that suggested Rafe Crosyer was near. I glanced around and, sure enough, he was watching me from across the way. He had a glass of dark red wine in his hand but I thought it was a prop rather than that he was really here to drink.

I told Scarlett I needed to use the ladies room and left the table. Rafe made his way in the same direction and when I was out of sight I turned to him, "What are you doing here?"

His wintry eyes lightened. "I might ask you the same question."

Of all the people to witness my humiliation, did it have to be him? There was definitely a vampire-to-human attraction between us but we'd always been too sensible to act on it. There could be no happily-ever-after with me and a vampire and I was vain enough that I didn't fancy growing old and decrepit while my partner remained eternally thirty-five. Nor, frankly, did I fancy becoming a vampire. So, Rafe and I remained something more than friends, and left the rest unexplored.

He said, "You look lovely tonight, by the way. You did all this for your date?"

I raised my hands in the air dramatically. And yes, I'd even painted my fingernails so there were ten flashes of red as I gestured. "It's that love potion. It's all gone terribly, terribly badly. All the wrong people are falling in love with each other. It was supposed to make Charlie fall in love with Alice. But, instead, Charlie seems to be in love with Polly, she's an actor in A Midsummer Night's Dream that Cardinal College is putting on."

It wasn't easy to surprise someone who'd been around for six hundred years. I think both of us pretty much thought he'd seen everything, heard everything and probably experienced just about everything. I had the dubious satisfaction of knowing I had managed to surprise him thoroughly. His eyebrows rose and an involuntary laugh shook his frame. "Wait. Stop. I thought you were going to ask Margaret Twig to help you. A novice like you shouldn't be messing about with love potions, not without supervision."

"What are you? My father?" I stared at him. "Of course we got Margaret Twig to help us. I didn't want anything to do with it. The love potion was Violet's idea. But, Alice seemed so sad and her longing was so real, that I thought perhaps we could help her."

Now Rafe looked puzzled. "You're not suggesting that Margaret Twig messed up the potion?"

"No. I don't know. I think Alice messed it all up. She had very specific instructions. She was to slip a little of the potion to Charlie and make sure that she was the first person he saw after he drank it."

"Sounds simple enough."

I was pleased he understood. "You'd think so, wouldn't you?"

I was starting to feel unreasonably annoyed. I hadn't made any mistakes with the potion but somehow I knew that Margaret Twig was going to blame me. Even Rafe seemed rather accusatory. "She brought the potion in a flask to the first meeting of the cast and crew of Midsummer Night's Dream."

He was gazing at me intently. "Why on earth would she do that?"

Who knew what had gone on inside Alice's head? "She told me that she can't get Charlie's nose out of a book when they're in the shop. It's true enough, I've seen him. Even when she brings him his tea and the fresh cakes she bakes him every day, he just eats and drinks and keeps on reading. So, she thought that in the rehearsal hall she could slip some potion into his coffee and get him to look at her since obviously he wouldn't be in the bookshop and he wouldn't have a book in front of him."

"And yet, her plan went awry. How astonishing."

Truer words were never spoken. I nodded. "Because she transferred the potion to a silver flask, a couple of the actors thought she'd brought alcohol into the room. Naturally, being boys, they each took a sip and then some fool tossed the rest of it into the communal coffee urn."

Slowly, he said, "That can't have ended well."

My hands waved about again. "That's what I'm trying to tell you. Charlie didn't fall in love with Alice, he seems to be infatuated with Polly. And the guy playing Lysander and the one playing Demetrius are now both in love with Scarlett."

He began to chuckle. "Don't tell me, she plays Hermia?"

I rolled my eyes. "I'm sure if Shakespeare were still alive he could write A Midsummer Night's Dream Two and it would be a big hit. Yes, she plays Hermia. I saw her take a sip of Charlie's doctored coffee. But I don't think she fell in love with him. I'm so confused." This was the hardest part to tell. "Then Ian arrived in the middle of the rehearsal and helped himself to coffee."

"Oh my, you're not telling me our noble Detective Inspector is afflicted with love-madness too?"

"That's exactly what I'm telling you. He's in love with Scarlett as well. That's why he stood me up. He took her to my beautiful dinner."

Rafe reached out and touched my bare shoulder. His touch was cool but oddly comforting. "I'm sorry."

I nodded.

"You know it's only the potion. It's a spell that makes people temporarily love addled."

I smiled slightly. Such a quaint term but very fitting. "I know. My pride is still stung, though."

"As it should be."

"So the whole thing is a mess. And as for Scarlett, half the cast and crew are now in love with her and I can't tell who she's in love with."

He chuckled softly. "My poor, sweet innocent. If Scarlett is that young woman who's been sitting beside you all evening, then Scarlett is in love with you."

I sucked in a sharp breath and slapped my hand over my mouth as the obvious truth of his words sank in. "Of course.

How could I have been so stupid? I tried to stop her from drinking Charlie's coffee and it was me she looked at after she drank it. And instead of looking at Alice, Charlie looked at Scarlett and then Polly, but I think he ended up fixated on Polly."

He looked more amused than ever. "Oh, what fools these mortals be."

CHAPTER 11

"It's a complete disaster," I said to Margaret Twig the next day. Her eyes widened as I recounted the mess the potion had made. "Jeremy's in love with Alice. Miles is in love with Scarlett and Charlie, who was supposed to fall in love with Alice, is crazy about a girl named Polly."

"Good heavens," Margaret said, her eyes crinkled in what I thought was amusement but might simply have been confusion. "And what about Scarlett? Is she in love with one of the actors?"

I felt myself blushing. "No. Scarlett's infatuated with me."

Margaret's chuckle was evil. There was no other word for it. It was exactly my idea of a witch's cackle only low and muffled, which somehow made it sound more devilish. "It's like an entire flock of baby birds have hatched and imprinted on the wrong mothers. Oh, dear, what a tangle."

I was so pleased someone found this fiasco amusing. Okay, two someones, since Rafe had clearly enjoyed hearing about the potion mix-up. I certainly didn't.

Cardinal Woolsey's was closed Sundays but I'd gone

down this morning to catch up on paperwork and nearly jumped out of my skin when Scarlett banged on the door completely ignoring the closed sign. It was awkward and embarrassing having her stare at me like that, knowing she was under the influence of a magic I'd helped create. Finally, I'd had to tell her I had an appointment. She only left when I promised I'd see her later at rehearsal.

I'd driven straight to Margaret Twig's house to ask for her help, though I wondered why I'd bothered if all she was going to do was laugh at me.

"There's something I don't understand," I said.

"Oh, more than one thing, I suspect."

I grit my teeth and continued, "We put Charlie and Alice's hair and blood in the potion. Wasn't that so they'd fall for each other?"

"Yes, but it doesn't make them immune from falling for other people, or others from falling for them."

"But why did Scarlett fall in love so strongly with me?"

The older witch shrugged. She was all in purple today, so she looked like a know-it-all grape. "One of your hairs may have floated into the mix, or just some of your energy. You have to be very careful when mixing spells and potions to remain completely detached. We work magic, but we mustn't put ourselves into it."

Now she told me. "So, the fact that I was invested in seeing Charlie and Alice get together means I could have put some of my own energy into the love potion?" I was horrified that I might have somehow polluted it.

"It's possible. As I keep telling you, Lucy, magic is an inexact science."

"I know, I know, that's why they call it magic."

She chuckled some more. "Exactly."

"Well, I now have Scarlett stalking me. I'm serious. She came to the shop this morning. I wish I worked in a high level building where you need security clearance to enter, but, sadly, a knitting shop is pretty much open to everyone."

"Oh, dear. Does she know you live above your shop?"

My eyes widened in horror. I hadn't thought my lovesick friend might try to break into my home. "I don't know. I can't remember if I told her. I might have. Before I realized."

Margaret tapped her thin fingers against the granite counter top of her kitchen. "You might want to stay with a friend for a few nights. Until the spell fades."

"Two nights, right? You said this wouldn't last more than three days and we've already passed twenty-four hours."

She sighed and shook her head. "How many times must I tell you? Not science. Inexact." She spoke the last words slowly as though I might be having trouble grasping the concept. Oh, and I was.

"You mean, you have no freaking clue when this spell will wear off?" I think my voice might have gone shrill for her eyes darkened in annoyance.

"You did ask for my help. I cannot be held responsible for the incompetence of novice witches."

I thought I'd better leave before I said something I regretted and she retaliated by turning me into a frog.

"Leaving so soon?" she called behind me as I marched back down the flagstone hallway to the front door.

Before I got there, I turned. "Is there an antidote?" It wasn't only the people in the play and Alice and Charlie who were affected. Poor Ian could end up harming his career if he acted toward Scarlett the way she was acting toward me.

Margaret had followed me down the passage, probably to make certain I left. But at least she answered my question. "The spell can only cause infatuation, not real love. True love will always be more powerful."

Which helped not at all. Only Alice would remain unaffected, because she truly loved Charlie.

I suppose I now knew one more thing. Whatever Ian felt for me, it wasn't love.

I PUT myself and my thoroughly broken ego into the small Ford and drove down the winding road that led me back toward Oxford. I pulled over before I got into town and texted Vi to see whether she could meet me at the shop to get things organized for the upcoming week. I didn't really need her, but I wanted to tell her what Margaret had said and see if she had any ideas.

Vi met me at the shop and I told her what had happened. All of it, from my date ditching me to pursue Scarlett to realizing that the woman he wanted, wanted me. At least Violet didn't think it was funny. But then she must be feeling as guilty as I was. Maybe more as the potion had been her idea.

When I told her about my fruitless trip to see Margaret, she nodded, not looking surprised. "I didn't think she could do much." She seemed to be deep in thought. Finally, she said, "Maybe we should try again."

"Try again?" She couldn't possibly mean...

"Alice can't have put all the potion in that flask. If there's some left, we could give the potion to Charlie again, this time when there's no one around but Alice." She went on, "And you could invite Ian for coffee and slip some into his cup."

I was not about to drug a man in order to get him interested and I was about to tell Violet that when the door of Cardinal Woolsey's burst open and the normally cheerful welcoming bells sounded like they were throwing a hissy fit.

I couldn't believe I'd forgotten to lock the door behind Violet and dreaded to see Scarlett, but it was Alice standing there. She was vibrating with negative energy and for a moment I saw a haze of red around her before I blinked and focused more carefully on her face. It was red and blotchy and her eyes had that swollen look of a recent crying bout.

Violet and I both rushed forward. "Alice, what's wrong? Are you all right?" I asked and in the exact same breath Violet cried out, "What's happened? It's not Charlie, is it?" So our mixed words collided in mid air sounding as discordant as the door chimes had.

Alice looked from one to the other of us. "I'll do it," she said. "I'll teach your knitting classes." And then she huffed a quick breath in and out. And all in a rush she said, "And I see from the notice in the window that you have a part-time position here. I would like to apply for it. I'm very good with customers, and very patient, I'm never cross, never late, and —" Here her voice became almost completely suspended by tears. "And I make a very nice cake."

Alice and I glanced at each other and without a word being said she strode forward and locked the door. "Come upstairs," I said. "Let me make you a cup of tea."

I was becoming so English that tea was the first thing I thought of in any difficult situation. Though, if her drama was bad enough, I also had chocolate and hard liquor upstairs in my flat.

Alice was wearing one of her homemade jumpers in a dull green. I knew for a fact that she had knitted her sweater several sizes too large because I'd rung up the purchase of pattern and wool. When I questioned her she'd said she liked to be comfortable. Comfortable it might be, but no one could deny that the sweater made her look rather frumpy, even though it was exquisitely knitted. She wore it with a skirt that was neither short nor long but hovered about her knees as though undecided which way to go. She also wore thick black stockings and orthopedic shoes far too old for her young years.

I put the kettle on, and Vi fetched a box of tissues. Then we sat around my kitchen table while her tale poured out. "I quit." She said the words defiantly, then blew her nose with resolution. She straightened her spine, folded her hands in her lap and said, "I made a dreadful mess with that love potion. I never should've asked for it. And now look what's happened? All sorts of people are in love with the wrong ones. Charlie's completely infatuated with Polly and one of those stupid boys who made the mess in the first place is in love with me."

"I'm so sorry."

She shook her head and blew her nose. "Jeremy Booth says I'm the most beautiful woman he's ever seen and he keeps trying to give me his school ring."

"It is a tangle," I admitted, "But it's not your fault. We never should've done it. However, the woman who made the love potion promised us that it wouldn't last longer than three days."

"I don't care. What this fiasco has taught me is that Charlie will never love me. If he'd looked at me once in the last three years the way he looks at Polly it would have been enough. I would've had hope. But he never has. And now, he never will. I thought I'd give it one more chance." She plucked another tissue from the box and began to shred it.

"I went to his flat this morning determined to speak to him. No tricks, no cake, no silly love potions. I would tell him as an adult about my feelings for him and ask him if he felt there was any hope of his reciprocating my affections."

I had a very, very bad feeling about this. "Alice, perhaps you should've waited until the potion wore off."

She shook her head firmly. "I've come to the end of my rope. I had to know."

Violet looked at me and grimaced. "What happened?"

"He wasn't in the flat. He was in the shop speaking on the phone. It was Mrs. Bradley, who was putting in a preorder for Martin Hodgins' latest novel. Naturally, I was pleased as the book is for her grandson who has been a reluctant reader. While he was speaking to her, I noticed he'd been working on the computer. I walked around behind him to see what he was doing and he was on that woman's Instagram account."

"Whose Instagram account?" Violet asked looking confused.

"Polly's of course. I didn't even think Charlie knew what Instagram was. I rather thought the entire concept of social media had passed him by. The photo he'd been looking at was of Polly and him at rehearsal. And the way he looked at her..." She shook her head. "I've never been a woman of violence. I didn't know I had a violent impulse in my body.

But I wanted to throw that computer across the room with all my might. I didn't, of course."

Nyx, who'd been sleeping on the living room sofa padded into the kitchen to see what was going on and immediately jumped onto Alice's lap. Nyx is a great comfort in times of stress. Alice stroked her, calling her a sweet puss, which Nyx took in good part, in spite of the fact that Alice left bits of shredded tissue in her fur as she stroked the cat.

Alice continued, "When he was off the phone, I cleared my throat and told him that I had something serious to tell him. He barely looked at me. He showed me more pictures of him and Polly on the computer and told me he'd never felt like that about a woman in his life."

"Oh, dear," said Violet. Nyx nestled more deeply against Alice and I poured more tea.

"So, instead of declaring my love I told him I was quitting." She gave a watery chuckle. "At least that finally got his attention. He looked as though I'd stabbed him in the heart. He said, 'You can't leave. What's the matter? Aren't you happy? Do you want a raise?'"

Violet looked at me sideways and said, "A raise would be nice. Who doesn't want a raise?"

"We're talking about Alice, not you," I said in a low voice. I thought that Violet was overpaid as it was considering the way she kept interfering in my personal life. And she didn't bring me fresh baked cakes every day, either.

Alice shook her head. "I don't care about the money. I inherited some money from my grandmother and I have a talent for stocks. My portfolio pays me all I need. I only work for Charlie because I love him. And, of course, I need something to do all day."

Violet's eyes widened. "Perhaps you could give me some tips. I'd love to have a stock portfolio."

"Violet. We're here to help Alice," I reminded her.

She tossed her rainbow striped hair over her shoulder. "Right. So, what did you say after he offered you the raise?"

She put her head in her hands and there was a moment of complete silence. Then, in a small voice, that emerged through her partly open fingers she said, "I told him I loved him and that I couldn't stay another minute, and then I ran out of the shop." She took her hands away from her face. "I didn't even stop to pick up my coat or handbag. One of you will have to go back and get it. I can never set foot inside that shop again. Anyway, I ran straight here."

I imagined what my grandmother would say in a moment like this. I had certainly come running to her with my share of problems and as though she were beside me guiding me I leaned over and rubbed Alice's knee lightly. "You did exactly the right thing. I'll go myself and get your bag and coat and demand he write you a check for whatever he owes you in salary."

"Thank you."

My cell phone buzzed. I checked it and then let the call go to voicemail. Vi raised her eyebrows. "Let me guess, the groveling detective?"

"Who knows if he's groveling? Maybe he's calling to tell me he can never see me again as he's in love with Scarlett." I rolled my eyes. "As if I care."

Both women looked at me with sympathy and Alice said, "I'm so sorry I ever started this love potion nonsense."

"It wasn't your fault. Anyway, my second assistant, Meri, is going on an extended visit to Egypt. You can take her place and we'll begin advertising right away for your knitting classes."

She looked fearful and grateful at same time. "Thank you. And you won't tell Charlie where I am."

I rather thought he'd guess but I didn't say so.

They both looked at me. "Are you going now?" Violet finally asked.

"Of course not," I cried. "The last thing I'm going to do is rush up there and immediately let Charlie know where Alice is. No. Let him feel what it's like at Frogg's Books without her. Let him manage the back orders and the mothers who can't make up their minds which books to buy their children for their birthdays. Let him make his own tea for once." I raised my eyebrows and looked directly at Alice. "Let him eat shop-bought cake."

For the first time since she'd arrived I caught the gleam of a smile. "He hasn't eaten shop cake in so long it might kill him."

It wouldn't do that, but living without Alice even for a day might show him what he was missing. It was entirely possible that nothing, not a potion, not Alice's efficiency and endless devotion was going to make him fall in love with her but she'd still be better off knowing that was the case than continuing to hope and dream.

I stood up and said briskly, "Right. Tea break is over. Violet, can you show Alice how to run our cash machine and how everything works? This is a perfect opportunity, while the shop is closed." I felt very profoundly that Charlie's loss was my gain as I said, "And I am going to start organizing our classes."

Alice immediately looked as though she had made a

terrible rash decision. "Must you plan the classes quite so soon?"

"Yes." I said it quite firmly because I knew that given half a chance she would find a hundred excuses why she couldn't teach the classes. The truth was, having eight or ten knitters sit around a table in my back room while she taught them to knit would be very good for her confidence as well as giving her something else to occupy her mind.

I may have sounded like a cruel taskmaster but I decided to be quite gentle in easing Alice into teaching classes. I added one beginner class to the website. We'd start there. I asked her if she was available on Wednesday evenings and, rather sadly, she said she was available every evening. I settled on Wednesday as it didn't conflict with the more regular use of my back room by the vampire knitting club. And, we'd see how she did before I added more classes.

Since I already had a waiting list of people who'd asked about classes I immediately began phoning them. I also put a note in my front window. Within an hour I had six people signed up. If I added myself that would be seven.

I went out front to tell Alice the good news and she seemed both pleased and terrified. I said, "We'll start next Wednesday. That gives you lots of time to plan but not very much time to get nervous. Honestly, they're all nice people who come here. And you're doing them such a favor."

"I did used to enjoy teaching knitting."

Just before three o'clock I walked up to Frogg's Books. I deliberately didn't tell Alice where I was going because I didn't want to be charged with a load of messages for Charlie that I had no intention of delivering. Much easier if I just walked over, grabbed her things and left. Obviously, he'd work out where she was from the fact that I was the one who'd come to collect them.

Unlike me, Charlie opened on Sunday afternoons and I was curious how he was making out without his faithful assistant. Sure enough, when I arrived, the man who usually had his head in a book and a fresh cup of tea at his elbow looked to be in a state bordering on dementia. I paused just inside the door and decided to enjoy myself for a moment on Alice's behalf.

"I'm sorry, I just don't know where it is," he said, and from his tone it was clear this wasn't the first time he'd said those words.

Standing beside him was a woman who looked irritable and overbearing. She said, "But why on earth would you phone me to tell me my special order was in if you didn't know where it was?" I felt that this was not the first time she had said those words, either.

Almost pleadingly Charlie said, "But it wasn't me who phoned you."

"No, it wasn't. Where is that nice young woman who usually helps me?"

And wasn't that the question. I waited with interest to see what Charlie would say. He looked harassed and helpless and finally said, "She called in sick today. She is not well."

The woman raised her hands in the air. "Can you call her at home and find out where my book is?"

He said, "Look, just give me a minute. It'll be in the back room somewhere."

She let out an exclamation of impatience. "Oh, never mind. I'll come in again later in the week."

She walked very purposefully out the door, nearly

colliding with me. Charlie looked overwhelmed and bewildered as he turned to me and then said, "Oh, thank goodness it's you, Lucy. How can I help you?"

"I just came to pick up Alice's things. She left without her coat or handbag."

He looked behind me and out to the street as though Alice might be hovering there. When he obviously didn't see her he looked disappointed. "I can't believe she just walked out on me this morning. It's been chaos."

I bit my tongue before I could say, "Poor baby," and murmured sympathetic noises.

"So, she went to you did she? I didn't think she'd gone far, not without her coat or any money."

I didn't think it was right that he keep telling his customers that Alice was sick so I said, as gently as I could, "I've given her a job."

For a man I would call mild-tempered Charlie took an angry step towards me looking furious. "You did what? You stole my best employee? That's not very neighborly of you."

"Alice told me she quit."

"Well she can't quit. I refuse to accept her resignation. Or, at the very least, I demand two weeks' notice."

I shook my head. "Come on, Charlie. You know you're not going to do that. She's upset."

He slumped into one of the cozy chairs he kept for customers and said, "Well, I'm upset, too. Honestly, I don't know what's got into Alice. She just announced she was leaving, without any proper explanation, or warning."

Had he not heard Alice? Perhaps I was marching in where angels would fear to tread, but I did feel involved in this romance, such as it was. I was the one who'd organized the love potion after all. I said, "Charlie, Alice has feelings for you. You can't expect her to keep working here day after day when you don't return her regard."

He crossed his arms over his chest and looked quite huffy. "What do you mean I don't return her regard? I think very highly of Alice. She is a most efficient woman, makes excellent cakes, is never late and all my customers think the world of her."

I couldn't help but smile. "Well, if I was looking for a recommendation from her previous employer, I guess I just got one."

"This is ridiculous. She doesn't want to work for you. She's happy here."

"If she's so happy, why did she quit?"

"Because she's irrational."

"Because she loves you?"

He shook his head, looking sad. "She's been here three years. It's never stopped her before. I blame this time of the year. Valentine's and all that nonsense." He waved a hand around. "Look at that. She's made an entire display of love stories. On the front table, right near the door. They're all there, the Brontës, Jane Austen, Shakespeare's love sonnets and a load of modern books that I certainly never ordered all covered in pink jackets. I ask you. No wonder it's made her suddenly romantic. As soon as February is over I'm sure this momentary madness will pass."

All I could think was poor Alice. Not only did Charlie appear not to return her feelings, he didn't seem to have any respect for love at all. I said, "I'll take her things now. If you let me know when her final paycheck is ready, I'll come and pick it up."

"Why can't she get it herself?"

"I don't think she wants to come into the shop." Though, presumably they'd be seeing each other at today's rehearsal of the play.

"Tell her I'll mail it," he snapped.

CHAPTER 12

When I returned to the shop it was to find Violet staring at Alice and looking eager. I did not like it when Violet looked like that. Her last bout of eagerness had ended in the love potion fiasco. And every time she forced me to one of the coven's potlucks or solstice events I seemed to make a fool of myself. I much preferred Violet when she was yawning and pretending to tidy the shelves while really checking her watch to see how soon she could go home.

Meri was a much more efficient assistant but, sadly, Meri was going back to Egypt with Pete. I'd seen the way they'd looked at each other and I suspected that if she came back at all, it wouldn't be to work in my shop.

Alice was tidying the mohair section and looking distressed. Before I could ask what was going on, she saw her coat and handbag in my arms and asked, eagerly. "How was Charlie? Does he miss me?"

I couldn't lie to her. "He misses your efficiency. He doesn't seem to know where you keep the special orders when they come in, and he nearly had a temper tantrum when he found out I'd given you a job."

She looked delighted and clasped her hands to her heart. "So he does care."

"Honestly, I think he misses his efficient assistant. Which isn't to say he won't end up realizing that he cares for you. But you have to give him time."

"And a makeover," Violet said quite firmly.

No wonder she'd been looking so eager. "What's all this about a makeover?" I asked.

Before Alice could speak, Violet said, "I've been telling Alice how pretty she is. But she doesn't make the most of herself. With decent makeup, a new hairstyle, clothes that actually fit, she'd be a knockout."

Alice blushed and shook her head. "But that's not me. I want Charlie to love me for who I am, not what I look like."

Violet looked impatient. She put her hands on her hips and said, "Lucy. Tell her."

I was certainly no expert in the whole male-female thing but I did have an opinion. "I think Alice is right. We need to feel comfortable with who we are. The man who loves us should see us as we are."

Alice looked happy and Violet looked petulant at my words. I continued, "However, I do think you might try wearing a sweater that's the right size. I'm sure you can find something that's comfortable and looks less... baggy."

Violet clasped her hands in front of her. "Please. Oh please, just do that." She ran to the rack where we kept completed sweaters that were for sale. Since my vampire knitters were so quick with the needles I always had a good selection. Violet flipped through them.

She glanced at Alice and then at the sweater in her hand. She checked its size and nodded. "Try this one." It was a simple black sweater with a scoop neck in the softest cashmere. The garment wasn't tightfitting or revealing in any way but it was stylish. Sylvia had knitted that one, so I knew it would be exceptional.

"Oh, I don't know," Alice said, but when Violet handed her the sweater and her hands touched the beautiful softness she said, "Well, maybe I could just try it on."

I sent her into the back and we waited. When she came out we both nodded, enthusiastically. "That looks great on you," Violet said. I had to agree. It made her look young and stylish and hinted at a figure that I thought most men would consider spectacular. Both of us were too smart to comment on the figure-showcasing qualities of the sweater, though. We told her how flattering it was with her coloring and hair.

She looked at herself in the mirror and her eyes sparkled. "Yes. I love it. I'll take it."

I refused to take her money and told her it was a signing bonus for agreeing to teach classes.

She looked down at herself. "But it doesn't look very good with the skirt, does it?"

Violet shook her head. "Do you have some jeans? Everyone has jeans. Wear those. And boots or some decent shoes."

"All right. Yes."

Alice and I were supposed to go up to the college for rehearsal at four o'clock. I wasn't certain whether Alice would go, knowing that Charlie would be there but she was made of sterner stuff. She went home to change, Vi went off to have dinner with Lavinia, her grandmother, and I finished up my paperwork.

I'd deliberately left my cell phone in my upstairs flat so I wouldn't be tempted to check my messages. However, I could only be so strong. The first thing I did when I got upstairs to get ready to leave for the rehearsal was to check the messages. Sure enough, Ian had phoned twice. A stronger woman would delete his messages without listening to them.

I discovered I wasn't that strong. The first message said, "Lucy. It's Ian. I can't even explain what happened last night." He let out a noisy breath. "I hate trying to talk to you on a message. Can we meet? Just a coffee or something? Ring me."

Hardly groveling and if there was an apology, I hadn't heard it. However, I did hear the confusion in his tone and had to accept that part of this mess was of my own doing.

Still, I deleted both messages. In a couple of days, when the potion had worn off, then I'd talk to him, when I knew he was back to himself.

I COULD FEEL the tension crackling in the air when I walked into the rehearsal room. I wasn't sure if it was my powers as a witch that made me discern the strange tension or whether it was so bad anyone would've noticed. Alice and Charlie were as far apart as they could get. Charlie looked longingly at Polly. Miles was making a nuisance of himself over Scarlett and Jeremy was trying to talk to Alice. The jokiness and fooling about were nowhere to be seen. Charlie was speaking to Will and even though I couldn't hear his words I could hear that the tone was clipped and edgy.

I now understood why Ellen Barrymore tried to keep the actors from getting into romantic attachments with each other. What a bad work atmosphere it created.

When Scarlett saw me she came running over, leaving Miles in mid-sentence. "Lucy. I've been waiting for you. Can you run my lines with me? Please?"

I reminded myself that it wasn't her fault that she was acting this way towards me. She was under a spell, partly of my making, so I tried to be generous. I said I would. She ran back and Miles immediately took her aside and began speaking to her in a low voice and not, I was fairly certain, about the play.

Liam, the actor playing Puck came and stood beside me and his gaze followed mine to where the tableau of clashing male egos was taking place. He shook his head and quoted, "What hempen home-spuns have we swaggering here?"

I giggled. He was the perfect choice for Puck. Small and wiry, with a wicked sense of humor. I wasn't certain, but I thought I recognized him from the winter solstice event. That didn't mean he was a wizard, of course. He could just be curious. Still, when he gave me a wink, I felt nervous as though he might be perfectly aware that it wasn't the tensions of the play causing the bad atmosphere but a witch-concocted love potion.

Alice hadn't had any sort of makeover, but she had taken her hair down and brushed it into shining curls. With the correctly-sized black sweater and decent jeans and boots she looked better than I'd ever seen her.

Jeremy seemed besotted with her. He'd clearly used the same strategy to get Alice alone that Scarlett had used with me. He'd asked her to run lines with him. Charlie watched him with a strange expression on his face. I got the feeling that even if he didn't want Alice, he didn't think anyone else should have her either.

Beside me, Liam chuckled again. Then he rubbed his hands together. "Oh this is going to be a very fun production."

Ellen had come in quietly and was standing just in front of where Liam and I were. I didn't think any of the actors had spied her yet, so she watched the drama on stage that had nothing to do with Shakespeare.

After a couple of minutes she sighed, and started forward, her Chanel flats tapping as she approached the stage. Polly saw her first and came forward with her script in hand. "Ellen, I'm having such trouble with this scene. I don't understand why Helena is acting like such a wimp. Can I play her sarcastic?"

Charlie rushed forward, close enough that when Polly tossed her blonde hair over her shoulder, she struck him in the face. *Good.* "I can help Polly. Perhaps we could work on the scene together?"

Ellen shook her head. "Polly, you will rehearse with Jeremy, and try playing the scene a few different ways. I'm not opposed to a feminist interpretation, but let's see how it plays."

She turned and sought out Alex, who was never far from her side. I sometimes thought Alex Blumstein was Ellen's bodyguard as well as general dogsbody. "Ah, Alex, can you find Jeremy and Polly a quiet place to rehearse? And see what the costume department found in the way of costumes we can re-use, will you?"

When Polly and Jeremy left with Alex, Ellen continued splitting up the love-potion victims. "Charlie, you take the rustics to the main stage to work on their scene. Except you, Will, you stay here and work with Scarlett. Miles, you come with me. Lucy, can you run lines with Liam? We'll all meet back here in an hour." I was impressed at how masterfully she'd separated all the mismatched lovers. Ellen Barrymore was, indeed, an excellent director.

After rehearsal I probably would have gone home but Alice came up to me and said, "Lucy, a few of the group are going to the pub and they've asked me to come with them. I feel a bit foolish as I don't attend school here. I decided I'd only go if you went."

I could see that Jeremy was watching. It was pretty obvious who had invited her. "Do you really want to go?"

She said, "I have to stop being in love with Charlie. I know that. I've given him three years of my life and my affection and he's made it clear he doesn't want them." She looked over at where Jeremy was talking to Scarlett, though they were both watching Alice and me. "It will take me some time to get over him, but I'm determined to try."

I liked Alice and I wanted to help her move on so I agreed to go to the pub. As we were leaving, Scarlett came running up and grabbed my arm. "Lucy, you're not leaving. Oh, are you going to the pub? Perfect. Just let me grab my things." I was counting the hours until that stupid potion wore off. It certainly didn't seem to be lessening.

When we got to the pub I realized, with a sinking heart, that Charlie had decided to come along too. I didn't think it would do Alice any good to have to watch the man she loved flirting with Polly but I soon discovered that Alice was made of stronger stuff. Charlie came up to where the three of us, Scarlett, Alice and I were standing and gave us his most charming smile. And Charlie at his best was extremely charming.

"How lucky I am to find three gorgeous girls." He glanced towards the bar. "What can I get you?"

Alice said, not without a certain amount of pride, "Jeremy's already gone to get me a drink, thank you." And then she walked away. Charlie watched her go and I thought, whatever his feelings, he was not indifferent.

He mumbled something and then followed her. "Alice, wait. I want to talk to you."

She turned. "Yes? What is it?"

He seemed at a loss for words and then said, "I don't understand what's going on. You left me completely in the lurch. Please, can you at least come back to the shop until I find someone to replace you?"

Was he really that clueless? Alice made a sound of irritation then said, "No. I can't." And then she walked up to where Jeremy was heading towards her with two drinks in his hand. I didn't want to be the recipient of Charlie's moaning so I said to Scarlett, "It's my turn to buy you a drink. What will you have?"

She followed me to the bar and we both ordered a glass of red wine. I wasn't in the mood for anything fancy, and I didn't think she was either. Miles and Will came in with Polly and Liam. They were all laughing.

Naturally, all the talk was about the production. Miles kept trying to get Scarlett's attention. Scarlett was clearly more interested in talking to me. And Charlie seemed torn between trying to talk to Polly and trying to overhear every word Jeremy said to Alice.

That was difficult as Jeremy and Alice were sitting in the

corner, speaking in low tones, but he didn't miss the moment that Jeremy reached over and twirled a lock of Alice's hair around his finger. It didn't matter that we couldn't hear the words, it was pretty obvious Jeremy was hitting on her big time. She might still be in love with Charlie, but Alice was not immune to the attentions of a very attractive young actor. Her eyes were sparkling and she seemed perfectly happy with her company.

Miles looked around and asked, "Where's Daffyd? I thought he was coming."

"He's being fitted for his ass's head," Liam said. Then put on a Welsh accent. "His Welsh ass's head."

Then, as though he were Daffyd wearing his donkey head, Liam quoted from the play, "O kiss me through the hole of this vile wall! Look ye, Boyo."

And Miles, not to be outdone, put on an even more broad Welsh accent and answered, "Not going to lie to you, that ass's head looks lush. Wilt thou at Ninny's tomb meet me straightway."

Of course, we all laughed. It was impossible not to, and then Miles dug out his script so they could play the rest of the scene, adding every Welsh cliché they could think of.

When they'd done the scene, Miles said to Scarlett, "We should run lines together. I want to get our timing right in the scene where we get lost in the woods."

I thought he wanted an excuse to spend time alone with her, but they were also serious about doing the best job they could and so she immediately agreed. Miles said, "My phone's over there in my bag. Give us your number, and I'll call you later."

Scarlett took out a pen and wrote her mobile number on

the front page of the chunk of the script and then Miles tore off the corner and pushed it into his jeans pocket. "Ta."

Then Polly, no doubt fed up with Charlie talking to her and watching Alice, suddenly stood and said she had to go. She had studying to do and an early class in the morning. With a wave to all, she left.

Charlie didn't leave, as I'd hoped he would. He stayed, talking to Liam, but still keeping an eye on Alice. Liam seemed to be enjoying the drama. I was glad someone was.

After a while, Jeremy stood up and so did Alice. They both put their coats on. Alice said, blushing, "I'll see you tomorrow morning, then, Lucy."

I tried to remain casual as I said, "Yes. Bye."

Charlie took a few steps forward and said, "Alice? Where are you going?"

Jeremy immediately went into tough guy mode. "What's it got to do with you?" he asked, taking a step towards Charlie.

"Oh, no," I said. I did not like where this seemed to be going. Alice looked at me, just as horrified.

Charlie, who always seemed so laid-back and easy-going, stood to his full height and also took a step forward. "Alice is my friend. I don't want her to do anything stupid. That's what it's got to do with me." As he said the words he stepped closer until he was within striking distance of Jeremy.

Liam downed the last of his pint and said, "Not inside the pub, mates. Come on. Outside."

But it was too late. Jeremy shoved Charlie in the chest and then said, "Come on," to Alice. She looked at Charlie who seemed unable to believe this was happening. "I'm sorry," she said, then started to follow Jeremy. Charlie ran forward, grabbed Jeremy by the shoulder, swinging him around and then, I think to everyone's shock, hauled off and punched him in the face.

There was some kind of unwritten male code, I supposed, for even as Jeremy crashed into a table, and righted himself, looking ready to do murder, Miles, Will and Liam got between the two fighters and dragged them outside.

Alice cried out, "Lucy. What should we do?"

I shook my head. "I think we should let them beat each other silly. They've been spoiling for a fight all evening."

She looked as though she might cry. "But over me? I don't want anyone to fight over me."

Scarlett simply looked bored. "It happens to me all the time. Men are such fools."

CHAPTER 13

By the time Alice and Scarlett and I went out onto the street, there was no sign of the men. I thought perhaps it was just as well as Alice was clearly upset. She glanced around and wanted to know where they could be and what we should do. Scarlett and I exchanged a glance and then Scarlett said, "Don't worry. Miles and the others won't let them kill each other. The best thing we can do is go home and leave them to it."

Alice looked worried. "But—"

"Scarlett's right," I said. Neither of them looked to be the fighting types and, besides, I suspected Jeremy would be anxious to get home and ice his nose. He wouldn't want to spoil his pretty face and I was fairly certain that Ellen would be furious if she found one of her leading actors disfigured by a pub brawl.

Alice said, "I wasn't going to go home with Jeremy. I could tell that's what Charlie was thinking. What a cheek. He was only going to walk me to my car."

"I know that." We began walking towards Harrington

Street and I knew that if Alice drove home to her house where she lived alone she'd only worry and brood so I said, "Why don't you come and sleep at my flat tonight?" I grinned at her. "Then I'll know you'll be in time for work tomorrow morning."

"Oh, I don't know. What about my clothes?"

"I'm sure I can find something that will fit you. And I've got an extra toothbrush and some things you can borrow." I wasn't making the offer only for Alice's sake. I really didn't want Scarlett getting more attached to me than she already was.

"Thank you," she said sounding grateful. "I'm really rather upset."

We walked Scarlett as far as the Porter's Lodge at Cardinal College and then Alice and I walked back down Harrington Street to my shop and the flat above. We both glanced up at Charlie's windows, in his flat above Frogg's Books, but there were no lights on. Whatever he was doing, he wasn't home yet. Neither of us said anything and we continued on to my shop. I was happy to note there were no lights on in my flat, either, which meant my grandmother hadn't decided to pay a late-night visit.

I took Alice upstairs and made us both some cocoa. I found her a brand new toothbrush and some night things and then wished her good night.

But when I got to my room I felt restless. I was never sure where my human senses ended and my witch senses began, but one or both of them felt jangled. I didn't like conflict, and I didn't like boys fighting. Surely that's all it was that was bothering me.

I also didn't like the fact that my potion had caused all this trouble.

I was settling myself into bed when I received a text from Scarlett reminding me I'd promised to help her with her lines. She asked if I could meet in the morning as she was trying to be off book by the rehearsal that evening. Scarlett seemed rather competitive and, I suspected, wanted to be the first of the actors to recite their lines without prompting. Since I liked Scarlett and felt guilty about her crush on me I agreed to meet her at eleven the next morning at Cardinal College.

I would open my shop with Alice's help and then Violet and she could manage without me for a couple of hours. The curious feeling I had of unrest stuck with me and it was a long time before I fell asleep.

Next morning Alice and I were both heavy-eyed over our coffee. It was clear that she hadn't slept very well either. We both nibbled unenthusiastically on toast and then she suddenly said, "I wonder if I should go and check on Charlie. I'm quite worried about him. He's no fighter. What if Jeremy really beat him up?"

I thought Charlie had seemed well up to the fight, and she'd be far better to stay away from him and give him a chance to actually miss her. However, she was a woman in love so I said, "You must do whatever you think is right."

She obviously took that to mean I heartily approved of her terrible plan and looked much happier. "Yes. That's what I'll do. It's only across the road after all. I can pop over and be back well in time to help you open."

As soon as we had finished our breakfast and I had declined her offer to help me wash up the few dishes we'd made she went off to get ready and in a few minutes called out that she was on her way.

I showered and then tried to decide what to wear. It was chilly and damp outside and so I chose a cherry-red pullover that Clara had knitted me that I wore with black trousers.

I was downstairs early, tidying a little bit before we opened. At ten minutes before nine Alice came hurrying to the door and I let her in. She didn't look relieved about her visit with Charlie; if anything she looked more distressed than when she'd left.

"What's wrong? Was he badly hurt?" Perhaps we should have tracked the combatants down and forced them to stop, though I had trusted that Liam, Miles and Will would do that job for us.

She shook her head and looked near tears. "No. It's not that. He's not there."

I was confused. "Who? Charlie?"

"Charlie! He's not at home. He's not in the shop. Where could he be?"

I thought she was making a fuss about nothing. "He probably slept in. He might be in the shower. Maybe he's embarrassed and doesn't want to see you."

She shook her head again, impatiently. "He has a hidden key. When he didn't answer I used the key and went into his flat. Lucy, he's not there. His bed's made as though he hasn't slept in it."

I wasn't as panicked by this news as Alice was, but it was strange. "Could he have gone out for breakfast? Perhaps he got up early and went out for breakfast, or shopping, or maybe a run? Does he exercise in the morning?"

"I suppose. He could have. But it's very unlike him. Very

unlike him." She sounded truly worried. "I never should've gone to the pub last night. If something's happened to him, it's all my fault."

I took her shoulders in my hands. She was trembling. "Alice. Charlie is a grown man. He got into a very foolish fist-fight with an equally foolish actor. If you make a big deal about this you'll only embarrass him."

"But I think I should call the police and report him missing."

"No. He would never forgive you. If he doesn't appear by tomorrow, which I'm sure he will, then that's time enough to be talking to the police."

"But there's that missing girl, too. Maybe there's some kind of maniac murderer about and they've got my Charlie."

I rolled my eyes. "He could've been kidnapped by aliens, too. Come on. Pull yourself together. We'll keep an eye on his shop. I bet you anything he opens on time."

As it turned out, Charlie was ten minutes late opening the bookshop. I knew that because Alice spent those ten minutes running in and out of my shop like a crazed cuckoo clock bird. In and out, in and out, in and out. It was giving me a headache. Finally, she came inside and heaved a huge sigh of relief. "It's all right. He's opened the shop now."

I put the back of my hand on my forehead in high dramatic fashion. "Thank goodness. Now I can relax."

She didn't think it was funny. "It's not very kind of you to tease me. I had a shock."

"You're right. I'm sorry. Now," I said, seeing one of my regulars about to come in the front door, "Do you think you're ready to serve your first customer?"

VIOLET ARRIVED AT TEN. Forty-five minutes later I left Alice in her more than capable hands while I headed up to meet Scarlett. She met me at the Porter's Lodge and then we walked together to the theater wing. I asked her if she'd seen Jeremy or heard any more about the fight but she hadn't.

We had to switch on the lights when we went into the theater wing. This was why she'd chosen this time, of course, as there were no classes or rehearsals scheduled. She wanted to use the main stage so she could get a feel of her space. Privately, I thought she wanted to show off for me.

We had agreed that I would sit in the audience and she would act out her part on stage skipping over any lines that weren't hers. It was easy enough for me to follow along as her script had her own lines highlighted in yellow marker.

In the past, whenever I'd been inside a theater it was full of people and buzzing with the excitement of whatever performance was about to happen. Even here, during rehearsals, there'd always been the buzz of excitement, actors dashing back-and-forth, each with their own private dramas. The stagehands and set builders and painters and costumers popping in to consult with Ellen who seemed to effortlessly impose order on chaos.

As we walked in, the space seemed eerily silent and cavernous. In the gloom, the rows of empty chairs looked like gravestones. Scarlett switched on the lights and that helped but still a shiver crept over my skin.

She didn't seem as fanciful as I. She chattered about the costumes that she and Polly would be wearing. "I wasn't sure at first about the white, but Ellen and the costume designer wanted to give the idea of virginal maidens and, of course, Hermia and Lysander are supposed to be eloping so they wanted to give the idea of a wedding dress.

"I've never thought of white as my color, but I have to say the dresses are gorgeous and we get to wear these really pretty silver and gold sandals."

As she was speaking we walked down to the front of the theater. The stage was already set up for the rehearsal that evening. They'd brought in some already existing props. There was a fake stone wall and Theodore and his crew had already been busy. There were a few trees and painted back-drops. I was impressed at how much they'd done in such a short time. Scarlett settled me in a seat where I could see her perfectly clearly and she could hear me if I needed to give her cues.

She said, "This is a pivotal scene. This is where I, Hermia, come across Lysander who, when I went to sleep in the woods, was planning to marry me. I woke up and he was gone and now I discover he's transferred his affection to Helena. At first I can't believe it, I think he's making a joke. Helena can't believe it either, she thinks we're all making sport of her. The two men threaten to have a duel, not over me, over Helena.

It was fascinating to watch her. Even as she began to describe the scene to me I felt her take on the character of Hermia. Her voice became a little lighter and her movements more fluid. She flipped open the script to the page she wanted and I told her I would follow along and let her know any time she stumbled.

She walked up onto the stage, paused, closed her eyes, and then, as though waking from a nightmare, she rubbed her eyes and looked about her. "Help me, Lysander, help me! Do thy best to pluck this crawling serpent from my breast!"

I watched as she flitted around the stage almost word perfect. She was going to make a terrific actress. Even without proper costume, no other actors on the stage, and little in the way of setting, she was amazing. The Shakespearean language sounded like normal conversation when she spoke it.

When in the play Lysander spurned her, she ran forward to the rock wall and began to cry. I waited and waited for her next line, but it didn't come. I prompted her, "Why are you grown so rude?" But still she didn't speak. Finally I stood and called out, "Scarlett? Are you all right?"

She backed away from the fake wall. "Lucy. I think you'd better come up here," she said in a faint voice.

And then she fainted.

As she crumpled to the floor, I raced forward, running up the stairs and onto the stage. I dropped to my knees beside her. "Scarlett?"

"Scarlett." I could see she was breathing. I didn't know if she suffered from anything that could make her faint. I didn't see a medical bracelet on either wrist.

I looked around for a cushion for her head, water, something useful.

And then I saw him.

He'd been hidden by the wall.

Jeremy, that beautiful young man who only last night had been full of life, wooing Alice, lay there, pale as death.

He was dressed in part of his costume. At least he had a cape fastened around his throat over his clothes. He was on his back looking up through sightless eyes. I could see the red, swollen nose where Charlie had punched him and it looked as though one of his eyes had begun to blacken. A wooden sword lay by his side as though he had been slain in a duel.

It hadn't been a sword that killed him, though. Someone had brought in a few real rocks either as props or perhaps as models to paint from. One of them lay beside the body and it was streaked with blood. I was no expert in forensics but it looked as though he had been struck on the back of the head with the stone.

I left Scarlett and crept forward to Jeremy. I checked the pulse in his neck with shaking fingers but his skin was cool to my touch and no pulse beat against my trembling fingers.

I stood there not knowing what to do. Rouse Scarlett or call the police? I decided to call the police and ran back down for my cell phone. I hesitated on whether to call Ian directly or the emergency number. Then I heard the scream.

Scarlett had come to. The first time she had seen poor Jeremy her body had shut down in a dead faint; now she jumped to her feet, her hands clutching her chest, bent over and screaming.

I hit 999 for the emergency number and, over the sound of her screams, told them to come immediately. Then I ran back to Scarlett and held her in my arms while she sobbed. Over her shoulder I managed to call Ian.

"Lucy, I'm so glad you called. I've been trying to reach—"

"There's been a murder," I said, cutting him off. Then, I told him where we were and what had happened.

I helped Scarlett down the stairs and then we sat in the front row of the theater as though waiting for the play to begin.

"He's dead, he's dead, isn't he?" she moaned in my arms.

"I'm afraid so."

She jerked away from me. "I can't stay here. I can't. Not while he's lying there, like that. We've got to get out of here."

I soothed her as best I could, but shook my head. "Scarlett, we have to stay. I've called the police. They'll be here very soon but we have to tell them what we saw."

"I don't want to. I don't want to think about it. It was so horrible. Poor Jeremy."

I wished I could get her water but I didn't dare leave her. I wished the police would hurry up. I nearly jumped out of my skin when a voice said, "Scarlett? Whatever's going on?"

I turned and thankfully saw that it was Ellen. She was wearing a stylish camel colored coat and carried a large black leather handbag over her shoulder. She was stripping off her gloves as she came towards us, a look of concern on her face. Her eyes narrowed on my face.

"It's Lucy, isn't it? What's wrong with Scarlett?"

I wished the police had arrived first. I didn't want to tell this woman that one of her actors was dead. As it was I didn't have to. Scarlett raised her head and through her tears cried, "It's Jeremy. He's dead." And then she pointed up to the stage.

Ellen glanced at me as though checking to see that Scarlett was telling the truth. I nodded. She put a hand to her cheek. "Oh no." And then she went up on the stage to have a look. I wanted to stop her, certain that the police would want to keep people off that stage as it was a crime scene, but I had no authority here. This was Ellen's world.

She didn't touch the body for which I was grateful. Instead, she put her hands to her heart and quoted, "Good night, sweet Prince. And flights of angels sing thee to thy rest."

She stood there for a moment with her head bowed, looking down at Jeremy and then she turned and slowly walked back across the stage and down towards us. I saw that tears were streaming down her cheeks. She sat on the other side of Scarlett and took her hand.

"Have the police been called?"

"Yes." I said.

We sat like that, the three of us, with Scarlett sobbing helplessly in the middle. Finally I said, "Would you stay with Scarlett while I get her some water?"

"Yes. Of course. You're very kind."

Cardinal College had a water station down the corridor, close to the entrance to the theater wing, with filtered water and paper cups, though most students brought their own water bottles. I grabbed two paper cups and filled them each with water. I was making my way back to the theater when the door opened behind me and I turned to see Ian running in.

"Lucy. Tell me what happened?"

"Scarlett and I found him. It's Jeremy, one of the actors in A Midsummer Night's Dream. He's in the main theater on the stage. He had his head bashed in with a rock."

He looked at me with concern. "Are you all right?"

I was as right as anyone could be who'd just discovered a man in his twenties, murdered. I merely nodded. He rushed past me, clearly eager to get to Scarlett and I let him go. Then he turned. "Am I the first?"

"Yes."

"Can you wait out by the door and lead the police in when they get here?"

"Yes, if you can take this water to Scarlett and Ellen."

He came back and took the water from me. "I'll get your statement later."

After he left I poured myself a paper cup of water and drank it down thirstily. And then I went to the door and opened it and stood outside. I drank in great lungfuls of cold damp air. Soon I heard the sound of sirens and then two uniformed cops were striding towards me and behind them were a couple of paramedics holding a stretcher. I knew from experience that there would be plenty more police here soon. The forensics team would arrive. Probably the detective chief inspector, a photographer, the medical examiner and finally the corner. So much business over one who had died far too young.

Who would want to kill Jeremy? And why?

The potion. Had the potion driven one of the mismatched lovers to kill his rival? My mind went back to the night before in the pub—the altercation that I had assumed was nothing more serious than boys indulging in fisticuffs.

But Charlie hadn't been home this morning. He hadn't been home when Alice and I had walked past last night, either. I had pooh-poohed her concerns that he hadn't been home all night. But what if she was right? If Charlie hadn't been in his flat, where had he been? And did his night's activities have anything to do with Jeremy's murder?

CHAPTER 14

This wasn't the first time I'd been interviewed by DI Ian Chisholm after a murder, but it was the first time I'd felt guilty because I knew I was going to hold back information that could be important to his case.

The police set up an interview room in one of the small rehearsal rooms in the theater wing. Ian decided to interview Scarlett first and then me, since she was the first one to stumble on the body. Scarlett clung to me and begged that I might be allowed to sit in on her interview and, after thinking for a minute, he agreed.

To say our little threesome was awkward would be an understatement. Ian was obviously still crushing on Scarlett and, I imagined, hurt and confused by the way she'd so brutally dumped him when he'd taken her on *our* date. Then there was his discomfort over the fact that I was the one he'd jilted in order to take Scarlett to dinner. And here we all were together.

I wasn't certain if he realized that Scarlett had feelings for me, but the atmosphere was so uncomfortable I didn't suppose the air could be any thicker with unspoken yearning and confusion if he did.

Since I was partly responsible for this romantic mess, I was glad to sit in on Scarlett's interview if only to prevent Ian from making a fool of himself over her. He could not afford to let his potion-induced infatuation show while conducting a murder investigation. I might be annoyed with him, but I wasn't going to let him damage his career.

I had already told Ian that Scarlett and I had met at the Porter's Lodge, had walked into the empty, dark theater and how she'd discovered Jeremy's body. He had asked me if Jeremy had any enemies that I knew of, and, since Scarlett or someone would mention the fistfight the night before, I told him about that as dismissively as I could, making it sound like a couple of foolish boys getting into it because they both wanted the same toy.

In fact, that's exactly what I had thought, and if it weren't that Charlie hadn't been home last night when Alice and I walked past his flat, nor had he been home this morning, I would've said the fight and the murder were completely unrelated.

Now, I wasn't so sure.

In spite of what I'd said to Alice, I thought it was very likely Charlie hadn't been home all night. Guilt was my unpleasant companion as I considered how much at fault I was for getting involved in that love potion.

I now recalled, bitterly, that when Violet and I had arrived at Margaret Twig's house that cauldron had already contained liquid. Margaret had said there was nothing in the pot but distilled water, but I had no certain knowledge that she wasn't lying to me.

I had no idea why she'd want to spread a potion around that not only caused love madness but possibly inflamed lovers to the point that they would kill each other. However, Margaret definitely had her own agenda.

So, after Scarlett told Ian about finding Jeremy's body, which, when she told it, seemed a small aside to her own feelings of shock and horror, he asked her the same question he'd asked me. Did she know whether Jeremy had any enemies?

She began to cry again. And, after wiping her eyes and blowing her nose, she said, "No. Jeremy doesn't have any enemies. Well, maybe Miles, because they're often up for the same parts, but there's never been anything other than professional jealousy between them." And then she gasped. Looked at me. "Oh, what about last night?"

I knew better than to answer. Ian brought her attention back to himself asking, "What about last night?"

Scarlett leaned forward. "Jeremy was leaving with this girl, Alice, who's been helping with the play. Then Charlie, who's an assistant director, tried to stop him. I really don't know why."

She pulled at a tissue, tearing it. "I'd have said they both fancied Alice, but Charlie was hitting on Polly all night. Then Polly left and he didn't seem to know what to do with himself."

"Charlie didn't?"

"Right. So, then, Alice got up to leave with Jeremy. Charlie objected. As I said, I've no idea why. There was some pushing and shoving and then Charlie punched Jeremy in the nose."

Since I'd already told him this, he merely nodded. It explained the swollen nose and incipient black eye on poor

Jeremy. Leaving the bigger mystery of who had struck him from behind with a rock.

He made a couple of notes on the pad in front of him and then asked, "What do you know about Charlie and Alice?"

She shrugged and shook her head. "They're volunteers from the community. Charlie runs that bookshop on Harrington Street, across the road from Cardinal Woolsey's. But I've no idea why he was so upset about Alice, do you, Lucy?"

I did not want to be brought into it. I shook my head. "This isn't my interview."

"Nevertheless," Ian said, "Do you know who this Alice is?"

Oh great. Now Scarlett had chucked me in it. I couldn't pretend I didn't know. "As a matter of fact, I do. Alice used to work for Charlie at the Frogg's Books. But now, she works for me."

He looked up at me and I could see his detective's brain whirling. "When did you hire her?"

"Yesterday."

Again he looked at me, not Scarlett. "What was their relationship?"

I knew what he was getting at, but I wasn't going to tell Alice's secrets. I shrugged. "Alice was a shop assistant at Frogg's Books and I asked her if she'd teach classes at my shop. She's a wonderful knitter and one of my best customers." I was going a bit far putting her in the best customer category, but she certainly purchased knitting-related items on a regular basis. "Perhaps she wanted a change, because she said she was interested in working in my shop if I had an opening. As a matter of fact, I did. Anyway, she's very efficient."

He looked at Scarlett again. "You attended school with Jeremy. What do you know about him?"

She'd been staring off into the middle distance and suddenly said, "Will."

"I beg your pardon?"

"Sorry, I was just thinking, you asked about Jeremy's enemies. I know I said Miles, but really, anyone could see they would both do fine. Ellen gave them both really good roles. But Will Matthews was always second string. He's good, but not quite as good, so he was often overlooked in favor of the other two. Well, this play's a perfect example. He auditioned to be Lysander or Demetrius and instead he got stuck with the role of Snug the Joiner. I mean, if you're going to be cast as one of the rustics, Bottom the Weaver is a wonderful part. But she gave that one to Daffyd, a pimply boy from Wales. I know Will was disappointed. And he's Jeremy's understudy, so if Jeremy can't perform, Will gets to play Demetrius."

"Disappointed enough to kill for?" Ian looked disbelieving.

Scarlett's tears had dried up and she looked quite serious. "This may just seem like a college production to you, but it's Ellen Barrymore's last college play. She's determined it's going to be the best thing we've ever done. I know she's already inviting her contacts from the media and talent agencies to come and see the play. What chance does Will have to be noticed playing Snug the Joiner? She threw him a bone by making him the understudy for Demetrius. Now, if the play goes ahead, Will's the one who'll be seen by talent scouts and theater reviewers."

Out in the hallway I could hear someone crying.

Everyone who'd arrived for rehearsal or backstage work was being held and would be interviewed one by one. Forensics were still in the theater and had closed it off so everyone was being held either in the big rehearsal hall or outside in the corridor.

Ian tapped the middle three fingers of his right hand on the surface of the table we were sitting around and looked at Scarlett intently. "Was Jeremy very friendly with Sofia Bazzano?"

Her brow furrowed. "Sofia? What's she got to do with this?" And then she drew in a sharp breath. "Oh I see. Will took her for a drink and she was never seen again. And Will was jealous of Jeremy. You don't think Will killed Sofia do you?" I could see she was about to cry again. I pulled a pack of tissues from my bag and passed it to her.

Ian said, "I don't think anything. I'm merely gathering information. Could you answer my question please? Was Jeremy friendly with Sofia?"

She didn't answer right away. She wiped her eyes and seemed to be thinking. "I know he had a secret. I came across him, about a week ago, giggling and so pleased with himself I thought he must've been cast in a movie or something. When I asked him he said, 'Oh, should I tell you? No, better not.' And then he giggled some more, looking far too pleased with himself. Naturally, I was agog with curiosity and begged him to tell me what his secret was but he wouldn't. He said something rather strange. He said, 'Scarlett, my love, I'm going to be a star. If you're very good, I'll put in a good word for you.' And that was all I could get out of him."

"Do you have any idea what the secret could have been?"

"Of course not. I'd tell you if I did. I even asked the others.

Polly said he'd probably landed an agent. But then, why wouldn't he tell everyone? I would. Miles said he was just teasing me. Will said Jeremy had probably discovered a new hair product. I told you Will was jealous."

"So, Will was present when you asked about Jeremy's secret."

"Yes. So what?"

Ian shrugged. "Just gathering background."

I wondered if we were thinking the same thing. If Jeremy had landed an agent, Will would be even more jealous.

"What about love interests? Was Jeremy seeing anyone do you know?"

"There was some girl in London he'd go and see on weekends. I think that ended. When he saw Alice he went a bit crazy. Didn't he, Lucy?"

They both looked at me. "I never knew Jeremy before the play so I really couldn't say. He was definitely hitting on Alice in the pub last night."

Ian nodded. "And now we come to last night. Who else was in the pub?"

Scarlett knew these people better than I did. She rubbed her temple with the heel of her hand. Her emotional distress was easing, but she was still in shock. "I still can't believe he's dead. I keep thinking I dreamed it." She looked at me. "Lucy, did I really find Jeremy dead on the stage?"

I reached over and took her hand. "I'm afraid so." She clutched my hand and didn't let it go. I said, "But we have to try and help the detective inspector find out who did this terrible thing." Even as I said those words, I knew that if Charlie was the person behind this I would have no choice but to tell Ian what I knew. I also needed to remember that there were other possibilities. The best thing I could do for Charlie was to keep my mind clear.

And my ears open.

"I can barely think straight. The pub last night is another lifetime ago. A lifetime in which Jeremy was alive and laughing and trying to get Alice to go home with him." Her eyes were red from crying, but somehow it only added a tragic touch to her undeniable beauty. I thought that one day she would use this experience to draw from when she played some tragic heroine in London's West End, or Broadway, or even in movies.

Still, she'd clearly been fond of Jeremy and I knew she was trying her best. "We walked down together from the rehearsal, Lucy and me and Alice." She looked at me. "Did Polly come with us?"

"No. I think she came with Charlie."

"That's right. And then Liam and Miles and Will all came in together. Daffyd, the one playing Bottom, stayed behind to be fitted for his donkey head. I think a few other people may have come, but they weren't with us."

"What time was this?"

"About nine?"

"And then what happened?"

She looked helpless. "Lucy bought me a drink. Red wine, if you must know. We were just a bunch of mates sitting around the pub." Then Liam and Miles started messing about, they were having a laugh, because Daffyd, who plays Bottom has such a strong Welsh accent. They started doing his lines in broad Welsh accents.

"Of course, we were all laughing, so Miles pulled out his

script and they started doing the whole scene, adding every Welsh expression they knew. It was brilliant."

She closed her eyes. "Jeremy was in a corner with Alice and it was clear they were getting along very well. Charlie was chatting up Polly but spent most of the time watching Alice and Jeremy. I think Polly got fed up with it because she left. She said she had an early class to study for, but I know Polly's schedule. She didn't have any classes this morning."

"Who else left?"

She thought back. "Miles got a phone call. He walked away to take it." She dabbed at her eyes, though I think fresh tears had stopped now she was concentrating on the events of the previous evening. "He gets these calls sometimes. He's very secretive about them. I used to think it was Sofia ringing him. But, obviously it's not her." And then she began to cry again. "Oh, how can this be happening? Sofia missing and Jeremy dead? It's a nightmare."

But Ian's gaze sharpened.

"Why did you think Sofia was the one Miles was talking to?"

"I don't know. I thought she was keen on him, that's all. Miles is very hard to read. I could never tell whether he liked her or not. Anyway, obviously it wasn't her."

"Did he get the call after Polly left or before?"

She looked up and her eyes widened slightly. "After."

CHAPTER 15

Scarlett and I were dismissed. Between this bizarre case, and his messed up personal feelings, Ian looked very confused indeed. I knew how he felt. Between my guilt about the potion, my fear that it had made Charlie crazy and my equally confused feelings about Ian, I could barely think straight.

"Did Miles really get a call last night?" I asked Scarlett as we walked out into the corridor.

She looked at me. "Yeah. I wouldn't make it up." I hadn't even noticed, I'd been too busy watching Charlie and Alice and Jeremy.

"Don't you remember? He came back in looking like he'd eaten bad oysters or something. I asked him what was wrong, and he said it was his mum on the phone."

"Maybe it was."

She shook her head. "His mum and dad are on holiday in the Maldives. He must have forgotten he told me." I obviously wasn't getting the whole picture for she rolled her eyes.

"They're five hours ahead. It would have been the middle of the night for her."

One more difference between rich people and me. They knew the time zone changes between Oxford and the Maldives. "If it wasn't his mother, who was it?"

"How should I know? All I know is, he lied."

We walked out into the corridor and found most of the cast and crew gathered either alone or in small groups. Some were waiting to be interviewed and some seemed to be there just to show support.

Liam was standing alone looking as serious as I'd ever seen him. He beckoned me over. "Lucy, I don't know what to do."

I glanced behind me but Scarlett had drifted toward where Polly and Will were standing together. Polly was crying and Will had his arm around her. Scarlett went towards him and he opened his other arm and pulled her in too. Could he really be a killer? He seemed like a nice guy. Scruffy posh, but nice.

"What is it?" I asked Liam.

He slumped back against the wall and looked up at the ancient ceiling as though for inspiration. "I thought the fight last night was over. You can tell when blokes have worked off their steam."

It felt like he'd launched right into the middle of a conversation and my mind was still processing the interview with Ian. It took me a second to catch up. I dropped my voice. "You mean after you left the pub? Where did you go?"

"Only round the corner into an alley. Jeremy and Charlie went after each other again but you could see their hearts weren't in it. We let them flail about and bash at each other but it was a bit embarrassing. Finally, I stepped in and told them to break it up. I think they were relieved. Jeremy and Will and Miles headed back to the college. Jeremy turned around and called Charlie a few names on his way out but we all understood. He was the one with the bloody nose."

"What about Charlie?"

"To be honest, I think he was the better fighter. He may have felt a bit bad about the nose and was trying to let Jeremy get one in. He took a clip to the jaw that knocked him to the ground and that's when I stepped in. I thought, so long as both of them ended up with a visible bruise it wouldn't look like one beat the other to a pulp."

I shook my head. I'd never understand men. "So honor was satisfied?" I said it sarcastically but Liam took my words seriously.

"Yes. Honor was satisfied."

In spite of my sarcasm, I felt relieved. "So you saw the fight end? And you parted them?"

"Yeah. I even walked Charlie back to his place, then I went back to the pub."

"You went back to the pub?" I thought I'd be too embarrassed to show my face there for a month.

He grinned at me. "It's one of my favorite places to drink. I wanted to make sure everything was cool. If anything was broken or damaged I was going to make sure we paid for it so they'd let us keep drinking there."

He looked troubled and I didn't think it was about his reception at the pub, so I waited.

"Nothing was broken and they took it in good part. Truth is, we bring them a lot of business. So, I had another pint and then it was last call. I went back to the college." He glanced around to make sure no one was listening. He dropped his voice to little more than a whisper. "It was when I was walking towards my building that I saw him."

Instinctively I also spoke barely above a whisper. "Who."

His eyes looked sad. "Charlie."

"Charlie was on the college campus after you'd walked him back home? It must've been dark, are you sure it was him?"

He nodded. "He didn't come through the main gate. Well, they wouldn't have let him in if he'd tried. He came over the wall."

"Over the wall?"

"Sure. When you've lived at the college a while, you get to know ways in after the gates are locked. The full moon had passed, but it was still quite bright and I could see him clearly. He was walking towards the theater wing."

"No."

Liam looked truly distressed. "I don't want to get a nice bloke in trouble. Do I tell the cops what I saw?"

I wanted to tell him to hold his peace, but for all the wrong reasons. I returned his gaze and I'm sure my eyes were sad and serious as his were. "Yes. You have to tell them."

I felt a sort of buzz going through the atmosphere and looked up to see Ellen walking down the corridor. She looked pale but calm. She stopped at each group to talk quietly, or listen. She didn't stay long, but every group she walked away from seemed a little calmer.

When she got to where Liam and I were standing, Polly and Scarlett and Will walked over to join us. The director looked at each of us in turn. "How are you all doing?"

I was certain she'd said the same words ten or twenty

times by now, but it felt for the moment as though we were her top priority. Polly said, "Oh, Ellen, it's so awful. Poor Jeremy." And then she began to weep.

"Do you want a hug?" Ellen asked.

Polly nodded and Ellen put her arms around the sobbing girl. After Polly had calmed, she said, "This is a terrible tragedy, and obviously we will do everything we can to help the police solve this heinous crime." I was impressed. How many people can use 'heinous' in a sentence and not sound pretentious? Somehow, she managed it.

Scarlett said, "I don't know what to do, or where to go. I feel I want to stay here, where we can all be together."

"Of course, you do," Ellen said soothingly. "We all do. I'm opening the big rehearsal hall later so we can come together and share our grief. I've asked for some grief counselors to be available should anyone need their services."

Scarlett said, "I will, definitely."

Polly sniffed. "What about the play?"

Ellen shook her head. "It's too early to say. And in the end it won't be my decision. It will be up to the college. But I know that Jeremy would have wanted us to go on. Perhaps we can dedicate the play to his memory."

I was fairly certain that Ellen would have more influence than she was letting on. If she was already thinking of dedicating the play to Jeremy's memory, then she definitely planned to continue. Cynically, I imagined the tragedy would increase ticket sales.

And Will would get to play Demetrius after all.

I told Scarlett that I needed to get back to my shop and was relieved when she decided to stay with the other actors. Already, tributes of flowers and a couple of small cuddly toys had begun to arrive and the groundskeeper was helping organize them in a flowerbed beside the door into the theater wing.

I knew I didn't have much time until Liam told the detectives about Charlie. I didn't know what I could do for him, but I could warn Alice. At least, she would hear about the murder, and Charlie's possible role in it, from me. If she felt guilt-bound to tell the detectives about the love potion, I wouldn't try to stop her. My own guilt was too great.

As I walked down Harrington Street towards Cardinal Woolsey's I realized how much I'd grown to love it here. Not just the shop, but my customers, my friends, the vampires who met in my back room to gossip and knit, my grandmother who I loved so dearly.

If the police discovered that my love potion had incited someone to murder, I imagined I'd end up in jail. I hadn't killed Jeremy, but I would likely be deemed an accessory to murder. I certainly felt like one. It was like I'd handed a loaded gun to Charlie and then filled him up with rage. I hadn't meant to, I'd only wanted to help two lovelorn souls find each other and look at the mess I'd made.

Instead of finding true love, Charlie would likely end up in jail, and I knew Alice well enough to know that she would never forgive herself. In Shakespeare's hands, potions and mismatched lovers caused comedy and, ultimately, true love. In my hands the same elements were turning into a tragedy.

I was striding down Harrington now, determined to get to Alice before she found out from anyone else what had happened. As I passed Frogg's Books I shuddered and quickened my pace.

"You were gone so long," Alice said when I rushed into the shop. "Was Scarlett struggling with her lines?"

Alice was so kind, worrying about Scarlett's performance. Her world still intact. I could hardly bear to destroy it.

Fortunately, there were no customers in the shop, so I flipped the sign to closed. "Alice, I've got dreadful news."

She paled. "Is it Charlie?"

Of course in her obsession she never thought about anyone but Charlie.

"Yes." I took a deep breath. Encouraged her to sit down and then told her everything.

Alice remained silent, her eyes fixed on my face, growing so pale I was glad she was sitting. When I'd finished she didn't say anything. Her hands were clasped tightly in her lap. Then, very quietly, she said, "This is all my fault."

"No. It's not. It's mine and Violet's. We never should have sought a love potion."

"If Charlie did this terrible thing, it's not his fault. I'll explain that to the police. This is my doing."

The jails were going to be full if they imprisoned every one of us who felt guilty about this murder, and yet, in some way we were all guilty. Me and Vi, Margaret Twig, Alice and Charlie.

She rose and put her shoulders back. "Are the police still at the college?"

"Yes."

She nodded. "I'll go up now."

"I'll go with you."

"But, who will look after the shop?"

"Anyone having a knitting emergency will have to wait."

We gathered our bags and then I pulled my keys from my

bag so I could lock the door behind us. But, before we'd even got outside, the door opened and Charlie walked in.

"Charlie?" Alice and I both called out at once.

He looked rather surprised. Was it possible that he hadn't heard?

Then he grinned, in his usual self-effacing way and put a hand to his jaw, where a dark shadow of bruise was spreading. "Don't worry, it's only a flesh wound."

Then, when he saw our expressions, he grew serious. "I'm terribly sorry I acted so appallingly last night. That's why I came here, to apologize." His eyes were on Alice and, for the first time, I saw an expression in their depths that reflected the way Alice had been looking at him for the past three years. Was it possible that he had finally fallen for Alice, now that it was too late?

Or was this a clever act? Designed to make Alice and me believe he was innocent of Jeremy's murder.

He said, "Alice, I've been a dreadful fool."

She took a step back and said, "Charlie? What have you done?"

His eyes went puzzled and he gazed at me and then back to Alice. "I've come to my senses. That's what I'm trying to tell you." He stepped closer. "Could we go next door and get a cup of tea, and talk in private?"

Alice said, all in a rush, "Charlie, the police are going to be looking for you, they think you killed Jeremy Booth, and it's all my fault." And then she burst into tears.

An expression of shock crossed his face. "What's all this? Nobody killed anyone, though our egos both took a blow. It was bloody stupid, and I'm heartily ashamed of myself, but at least having a turn up with Jeremy seems to have knocked some sense into my head."

But Alice had her face in her hands. He turned to me and I thought if he was acting this look of utter bewilderment then he was better than any actor that Ellen Barrymore had trained.

I said, "It's true, Charlie, Jeremy is dead."

"He can't be. All I did was punch him in the nose. Who dies from a punch on the nose from someone like me?" He spread his arms and I had to agree he didn't look very buff. "I lift books, not weights. Honestly, *you* could beat me up. I only managed to hit him because he didn't see it coming."

But, for all his charm, Charlie couldn't change what had happened. "Jeremy didn't die from the punch on the nose. His head was bashed in."

All the color left his face so the bruise on his jaw looked suddenly darker and more ominous.

I knew that Ian would be furious if I gave Charlie all the details so I stopped giving information and started requesting it. "What happened after you left us last night?"

He winced, more from embarrassment I thought than pain. "Jeremy and I and four of the actors went round the corner into the alley and continued to make utter arses of ourselves. Then, Jeremy and Miles and the other fellow. Will is it? Walked back to the college, I think. And Liam walked back with me to Frogg's Books."

So far, his story tallied with Liam's. It was what had happened then that I really wanted to know. "Then what did you do?"

He glanced at Alice who'd taken her hands away from her face and was looking at him through tear-stained eyes. "Alice,

142

I didn't kill him. I wouldn't kill anyone." He let out a breath. "I just felt so confused. I thought I was crazy about Polly, but then, seeing you go off with Jeremy made me crazy. I couldn't bear to think of you with anyone else. And yet, I had these feelings for Polly. Honestly, I've never been so thick-headed. I couldn't settle. I'm sorry, Alice. You won't like this bit, but I walked up to the college. I thought, if I could talk to Polly, I could sort out my feelings. See if she had any for me, I suppose."

He rocked back on his heels. "Even though I'd only drunk a pint, and I don't think I finished that, I felt peculiar. Not drunk, exactly, but as though I was in a dream."

Oh how I wished I'd never heard the words *love potion*. Obviously, his dose had worn off, but had it done so in time? Had he done something in his 'dream' that he couldn't remember? Something horrible, like murder?

"I couldn't walk in the front gate, of course, as I'm no longer a student and it was late. But I remembered a spot where I used to be able to climb the wall and get in and, sure enough, I was still able to manage it. I knew where Polly's room was because we'd talked about her view. I told her which room I'd once occupied and she told me where hers was."

Alice looked very disappointed. "You went to Polly's room?"

He smiled, ruefully, and shook his head. "I only got as far as the front door of her building. And then it struck me how ridiculous I was being. I can't describe the feeling but as I stood there, under the moonlight, in the grounds of the college I'd attended a decade ago, I realized I was acting like a boy and not a man.

"I don't love Polly. I blinked a few times and I had strangest feeling as though I were coming awake. I looked around and I realized I needed to see you, Alice. I'd acted badly and I wanted to apologize and talk to you without everyone being around. So I turned around, climbed over the wall, and walked back to my shop."

He closed his eyes, as though he were in pain. "Then I got in my car and I drove to your place. I rang your bell, but you clearly weren't home yet"

Alice went red and then white. "You drove all the way to my house? And I wasn't there." She nearly wailed the last few words.

"No. You weren't. I don't care where you were. It's your business. And I was an absolute fool, and let you get away when you are the best thing that has ever happened to me."

"Oh, Charlie."

And then he looked quite puzzled. "Wait a minute. I waited all night, and you never came home. Weren't you with Jeremy?"

Her jaw fell open. "No! I wasn't with Jeremy. He was only going to walk me to my car. After you had the fight and Lucy could see I was upset, she invited me to come here and spend the night. I tried to go and see you this morning before the shop opened, but you weren't there."

"I fell asleep in my car waiting for you to come home." He rubbed his neck. "Got a dreadful crick in my neck, too."

"So, you were sitting outside in your car all night? In front of Alice's house?"

"Yes. Stupid, I know, but I fell asleep."

Stupid and really unfortunate if it was true. "Did anyone see you?"

"I don't know. They may have. Someone may have seen the car."

Oh this was not good. This was not good at all. Charlie didn't seem to be as worried about Jeremy's murder as he was about Alice. He reached out and took her hand. "You do believe me, don't you?" Then he smiled his very charming smile. "I think I went a little crazy when those rehearsals started. I saw Polly and I thought in a blinding flash that she was everything I'd ever wanted. You hear all that nonsense about love at first sight but I'd never believed it until I saw Polly. But, I don't love Polly, I barely know the girl. I began to realize, last night, that it's you. It's always been you."

I glanced at Alice and saw her eyes and cheeks begin to glow.

"You're there in the morning, always cheerful, you look after all the customers, know where all the books are." He patted his stomach. "I've gained about ten pounds on your delicious cakes. It just wouldn't be the same without you. I can see that I took you for granted. I really didn't see what was under my nose."

Alice snorted. "That's because you always have a book under your nose."

He chuckled. "Well, no more. If you will please come back to me, we'll start fresh. We'll be partners. Proper partners."

She wasn't completely certain yet. "You mean, partners in the book shop?"

"No. Partners in life. Alice, I'm asking you to marry me."

"Oh, Charlie," Alice said, and then he pulled her into his arms and kissed her, thoroughly.

She threw her arms around him and I averted my eyes and thought I'd better leave the closed sign up on my door when I caught sight of Ian and a uniformed police officer heading toward my shop.

"Alice. Charlie." It was all I managed, before Ian opened my shop door. I suspected he'd come to talk to Alice for his eyes widened when he saw Charlie.

He said, "Charles Wright?"

Charlie took a step away from Alice and straightened his shoulders. "Yes."

"You'll need to come to the station and help us with our inquiries."

Charlie nodded, looking resigned. "Yes, of course."

As they left, Alice ran forward. "Charlie..."

I put a hand on her shoulder to stop her following them. "They'll only question him. They won't arrest him without more evidence."

"So I'll see him again?"

"Of course you will."

"I suppose they'll want to question me, as well."

"I imagine so."

She bit her lip. "Do I have to tell them about the love potion?"

And wasn't that the thorny question. "Alice, I don't know. Jeremy didn't die of a love potion. If Charlie *had* killed Jeremy over you, then we would have had to tell the police. But I believe Charlie, don't you?"

She looked appalled. And said, quite scolding. "Of course I believe Charlie. He'd never tell a lie. Someone else killed Jeremy."

"Then, instead of worrying about the potion, I think we'd better figure out who did kill Jeremy."

CHAPTER 16

I'd given Violet the day off but now I phoned her and asked her to come in, telling her it was an emergency. I didn't care what she had planned, she could change those plans, since she was the one who'd thought up the stupid love potion idea in the first place.

A customer came in and Alice served her. She was doing her best to hold it together but her hands were shaking and when she went to bag the purchase she dropped one of the balls of wool onto the floor. As soon as the woman left I said, "Why don't you go home? You've had a terrible shock."

She shook her head vehemently. "I will not leave Charlie when he needs me most." And she turned to me, "Lucy, did I dream it or did Charlie ask me to marry him?"

I smiled at her. "He definitely asked you to marry him." *Right before he was hauled off by the cops.*

She sighed. "This should be the best day of my life, instead it feels like one of the worst."

I had to admit Charlie's timing could have been better.

She looked at me as though I had all the answers when I had none. "Lucy, I must do something. Tell me what to do?"

I understood that need to push forward for the truth, and, since she was helping with the play, she knew a lot of the cast and crew. There must be something she could do.

My mind was racing. "If Charlie didn't murder Jeremy-" I put up my hands to stop her before she burst into all the reasons why he was innocent. "And I believe he didn't, then we have to help the police discover who did. It was awfully bad luck that Liam saw Charlie on the grounds. But maybe if he saw Charlie, he saw someone else, too.

"Someone he wouldn't think was out of place so he wouldn't mention it." I was pacing up and down now, something I did when I was agitated and thinking deeply. "Miles and Will were the ones who walked back to the college with Jeremy. We need to talk to them. Did they take him right up to his room? We need to know every step they took from the moment they left us."

She looked puzzled. "But won't the police have already asked them all that?"

"Probably, but the police won't tell us what they've discovered. And, we are all friends because we're working on the play together, so the actors and stage hands and so on won't be so nervous talking to us. They might remember things when we ask that they wouldn't think of under the stress of police questioning."

"I don't know. I've never done anything like this, before." She looked uncertain. "I'd try to ask the right questions and make a mess of it."

I couldn't imagine what she was going through, so I suggested, instead, that she go back to the college and hang around the area where people were leaving tributes. It seemed the natural gathering place now that it had become an impromptu memorial garden. I imagined the drama students would hang around there and people would come and go. As people do at memorials, they would share their thoughts about Jeremy. Tell stories about how they knew him. Describe things they'd done together.

"Just listen," I said. "Whoever murdered Jeremy was there last night. They had to have a reason."

She was looking at me, intently, and I felt that she was memorizing my every word. Then her brow creased. "If Charlie was able to climb over that wall without having to go through the Porter's Lodge, couldn't some random killer have done the same thing?"

I was pleased that she was thinking strategically. "Yes. Good. You're thinking like a detective. Of course they could. But, even so, no one kills without a reason. Or a perceived reason. And the way that Jeremy was partly dressed for his role, with the sword by his side, strongly suggests that the murder was somehow related to the play."

Alice nodded. "Actors are terrible showoffs."

"I know. Will could've done it. Killing Jeremy and then putting him in the cloak, and leaving the sword by his side, could be an expression of his jealousy."

Her eyes clouded and she shook her head. "No. Not Will. He's so lovely. Will would never kill anyone."

I took her to task. "Alice. How many times has there been a murderer exposed on the television news and their neighbors and coworkers say what a nice guy they were? If killers went around looking evil and murderous all the time the police wouldn't have such a hard job catching them. You have to step away from your own personal feelings. Think of everyone involved in the production, not as your friends, or as people working on the play with you, but as possible suspects. They remain suspects until we can prove to our own satisfaction that they are innocent."

"Like Charlie."

I nodded. "Exactly. Like Charlie."

"Even though we can't prove that Charlie didn't do it?"

I leaned back against the wall of wool, appreciating the warm softness at my back. "Unlike the police, we don't have to go purely on facts."

I thought back on what Charlie had told us. "But facts help." I chewed on my lower lip. "Instead of going back to the college, I have another idea. Why don't you go back to your home, and take Theodore with you. "

Her eyebrows lifted. "Theodore?"

"When he's not painting scenery, Theodore is a part-time private investigator. Maybe get a picture of Charlie's car and showed around your neighborhood. See if you can find someone who saw his car parked out in front of your house. It would be even better if anyone saw Charlie go and ring your bell, then that proves he was where he said he was."

"Yes. I can do that." She looked pleased to have a project.

"Good."

I would have to rouse poor Theodore out of his slumbers but I was fairly certain he'd be only too pleased to help Alice. He enjoyed investigating and I knew he missed being a police officer. He was old school, too, since he'd been active long before computers and cell phones and modern-day forensics. He still worked on finding clues, and talking to people. Besides, he'd be good company for Alice.

While Alice went to take a picture of Charlie's car on her phone, I ran downstairs to wake Theodore. I just hoped I didn't wake all the sleeping vampires, because some of them could be very cranky if woken before they were ready. Also, they tended to wake up hungry, which sometimes made them eye me in an unpleasant sort of way.

However, I had my own sins to expiate and so I banged quite firmly on the old oak door. I wasn't wearing a coat and the tunnel was dank and chilly. Fortunately, I didn't have to wait long before the door was opened. To my surprise, and relief, Rafe was standing there, wide-awake and fully dressed. He didn't look very pleased to see me. "Lucy. I've told you time and again you shouldn't travel these tunnels on your own."

I appreciated his overbearing concern, but I'd been going back-and-forth between the vampires' lair and my shop many a time without ever encountering so much as a rat. Thank goodness. Once a bat flew by and I was sure if light ever penetrated this far, I would see spiders the size of dinner plates but since I'd never seen one I chose to ignore the possibility. "I'm fine."

Before he could tell me off, I told him I was happy to see him, which took him back enough that I was able to walk inside before he even started on his lecture.

"I need Theodore. Is he still asleep?"

"I think so. Why do you need him? Is there a scene painting crisis?"

"No. If you must know, there's been a murder."

His eyes narrowed on my face and then he nodded. "That's why I'm here."

"You already know about the murder?" I couldn't imagine how news had got to him so fast.

"No. I felt unsettled. I thought you might need me."

I tried to appreciate that he was very, very old and didn't mean to be chauvinistic and controlling. Besides, sometimes I did need him. There were times when an ancient vampire of high intelligence, superhuman strength, and a broad knowledge of human nature came in very handy.

"I probably do need you. I need to talk this through with someone."

"Who's dead, and are you in any danger?" He looked ready to tear the throat out of anyone who might be a threat to me.

I shook my head. "I'm fine." Then I told him, briefly, about Jeremy's death.

"Odd that he should be killed when that female student went missing last week. It's very strange to have either of those things happen at Cardinal College. To have two such incidents in a week strongly suggests a connection."

"I agree. I'm sure there's a pattern here but I can't make sense of it. I need Theodore to do some policing work."

"I'll go and wake him. Wait in the living room, I'll be right back."

I settled into one of the deep red velvet chairs. I'd been coming here often enough that the opulent surroundings no longer surprised me. I never got tired of looking at the art masterpieces that hung down here, though, including the van Gogh that brought the warmth of southern France into the chilly stone cavern. I heard the front door open and Alfred came in. He looked as surprised to see me as I was to see him. "You're late getting to bed."

He looked a bit sheepish. "Poker. Lost track of the time." And he rubbed his stomach. "I'm starving. Must eat before I go to sleep." Then he headed for the fridge in the kitchen.

Rafe came back and settled beside me. Before he could say anything, Alfred came back out looking peevish, his long nose quivering. "When's Christopher bringing the new shipment from his blood bank? There's nothing in the fridge but type O. It makes my tummy queasy."

Rafe shook his head. "You'll have to ask Christopher."

Alfred came closer to me and I did not like the gleam in his eyes. He said, "And you're looking most delectable today, Miss A positive."

Instinctively, I ducked my chin down and put a hand up to my throat. I liked Alfred and he was an excellent knitter, but hungry and with that look in his eye, I wasn't quite sure.

Rafe made a sound like a growl and said, "Alfred!"

Alfred waved him away, chuckling. "I was only joking, my dear. I never eat my friends."

Then he sighed. "Think I'll go visit Dr. Christopher Weaver and invite myself for a late supper. I'm convinced he keeps the best stuff for himself."

He waved and headed back out. Then Theodore came into the room, blinking sleepily, with his baby fine hair sticking up in tufts.

He was drinking his breakfast from an insulated coffee cup. He must've scrambled into his clothes for he was fully dressed in dark trousers, a cotton shirt and a tweed jacket. He could've been anything from an insurance salesman to a history professor at one of the colleges. I suspected he chose that outfit exactly for that reason, so he'd blend in.

My grandmother wandered out, yawning. Gran had

always suffered from insomnia and I felt bad that we'd woken her. Still, she seemed pleased to see me. "Lucy, what a lovely surprise." Then she glanced at the antique clock on the wall. "What's going on?" she asked. "Shouldn't you be in the shop?"

I briefly explained that I needed Theodore's help to do some private investigating. She nodded, glanced at Theodore and, taking a comb from her pocket, walked over and tidied his hair for him.

Theodore finished his drink and rose to come with me. Rafe said to my grandmother, "Lucy needs some help with her own investigation. I'm going up with her now to her flat, why don't you come too?"

Once more, he was being very high-handed, but it was a good idea to get my grandmother straight up to my flat so she wouldn't be tempted to wander into the shop and frighten my customers—especially those who had been to her funeral.

Also, I always felt better when my grandmother was around. She looked pleased to be invited and then said she'd better wake Sylvia or her friend would be very annoyed to have missed out.

I told them to wait until Alice had left, then Theodore and I travelled back through the tunnel that led to the trapdoor and into my back room. I went up first, even though I'd left the closed sign on the door. I always believed in supreme caution where the vampires were concerned.

heodore came up behind me and we closed the trapdoor and replaced the carpet before Alice was back.

Her cheeks were red with the cold, or, perhaps, emotion. However, she seemed delighted to see Theodore and, in spite of his assertion that he was bashful around young women, he seemed comfortable enough around Alice. Maybe, having been the unwitting love interest of a couple of infatuated stagehands, he found Alice easy company.

They agreed that she would drive to her house and the pair of them would canvas the neighborhood. Theodore, very sensibly, suggested that they show pictures of Charlie himself not just his car because, ultimately, we had to prove that Charlie had been far away from the scene of the crime, not his car.

Of course, much would hinge on when forensics determined the time of death to have occurred. I was no expert, but when I'd try to find a pulse Jeremy had been cold. He must have been dead for some hours when we found him.

Violet arrived shortly after Theodore and Alice took off in Alice's car. "Honestly, Lucy, it's a good thing you caught me. I was about to dye my hair. What's going on?"

I told her about the murder and Charlie and her eyes grew large and round. "You don't think the potion had anything to do with it, do you?" she asked in a small, scared voice.

"I don't know. But I sure hope not."

Violet was understandably pouty at being left to run the shop while I was able to do the more interesting job of sleuthing, but since the love potion had been her idea, she told me not to worry about the shop at all. She'd take care of everything, including closing up.

It was the least she could do.

She also told me that come next year she was going to volunteer to help with the local theater production. She'd have been welcome to have had my place this year, and to have found poor Jeremy, but naturally I didn't say so.

When the coast was clear, I opened the trapdoor and Rafe, Gran and Sylvia climbed up into my back room. The two women were yawning but, while Gran wore a flowered house dress Sylvia had dolled herself up in wide bottomed black silk trousers, a dark blue silk blouse and a cashmere stole. Her silver hair was perfectly coiffed.

They all had insulated coffee thermoses with them and once we got up to my flat I decided to join them and put the kettle on, and pulled out my French press, to make coffee. Gran came into the kitchen looking concerned. She touched my face with her cool fingers. "Are you all right, Lucy? You look as though you've had a shock."

"I did have a shock. I thought I'd be running lines with

Scarlett, not looking down on a man younger than myself who'd been murdered."

"You sit down, dear. I'll make the coffee." She opened the biscuit tin, which was seriously depleted, and said, "And I'll make you some more gingersnap cookies today. That always cheers you up."

When I got back to the main sitting area, Rafe and Sylvia were sitting side-by-side. Sylvia said, "You'd better tell us everything that happened."

"I'll have to take you back to last night." By the time Gran returned with my coffee and half a dozen gingersnaps on a plate, I'd caught Rafe and Sylvia up to date. I assumed that Gran had been able to catch most of what I'd said from the kitchen.

Before I'd had more than a sip of my coffee and a bite of gingersnap, the intercom phone rang letting me know there was someone at my front door. I felt puzzled as I wasn't expecting anyone, but I went and answered it. No doubt it was a delivery.

"Lucy? This is your great aunt Lavinia. I need to speak to you." Then her voice softened as though she'd turned her head away, "Yes, all right," and then her voice grew stronger as though she'd turned back to the intercom again. "I'm with Margaret Twig. She wants to come up, too."

I stood there with the phone in my hand thinking there weren't two people I less wanted to see at the moment. However, they knew I was there, and being witches, if I didn't let them in they'd find another way into my home, so I pushed the button that would open the downstairs door. It sounded as though they were arguing on the way up the stairs. I looked at Gran but she simply shrugged her shoulders and so we waited.

Lavinia burst in first, almost as though she'd elbowed Margaret out of the way. "Lucy, it's imperative that you not say anything about the coven or witchcraft to the police." She looked quite anxious. "You haven't, have you?"

I was in the middle of saying, "No. I haven't said anything, yet," when Margaret came in. Her cheeks were red and bunched up like crabapples, and her usual sardonic amusement was missing. In fact, she didn't look nearly like her usual dramatic self. She was wearing blue jeans that looked muddy about the knees, as though she'd been gardening and over top she wore an old sweatshirt.

She said, "I just heard. How did that potion turn deadly? What on earth did you do to it, Lucy?"

Before I could protest that I hadn't done anything, and if anyone was at fault it had to be her, she continued, "We can't allow you to practice locally if you're going to cause trouble. Lavinia's right. We practice our craft in secret. By bringing the public gaze upon us, and especially that of the authorities," she shivered as though the Spanish Inquisition was at the door, "You've brought great danger to us all."

Even as I dimly understood that she was trying to cast blame on to me so as to appear blameless herself, I grew angry and wanted to tell her exactly what I thought of her stupid potions. But Gran was ahead of me. She stomped out to face the two witches, her flowery chintz house dress flapping and, for the first time ever, I realized at a visceral level that my grandmother was a vampire.

She seemed taller, stronger, and very angry. I didn't see her face, but both the witches took a step back. Gran said,

"Don't you ever come in here and speak to my granddaughter like that. Lucy is trying her best to respect the craft, and learn it in a sensible, controlled fashion." That wasn't exactly true, but I appreciated the support.

Lavinia sputtered, "Sensible!? Controlled? She all but destroyed our circle of sacred standing stones. She sent the main stone shooting through the air like a SCUD missile. What's sensible about that? It was reported as a UFO."

"That's because of you two, always pushing her. Of course she's powerful, and when she's finished her training Lucy will be the most powerful witch in Oxfordshire." Gran glared at Margaret when she said those words and, to my surprise, Margaret Twig nodded looking quite abashed. "So, if you have come here, it better be to help us find a solution to this problem and not to cast blame where it does not belong."

"Yes, Agnes," Lavinia said, sounding much more subdued.

Gran said, sounding much more like her normal self, "Good. Then, if you're ready to be sensible and help us you may come in and have some coffee."

They came all the way into the sitting room and when they saw Rafe and Sylvia sitting there they seemed a little shaken. I didn't blame them. If there was a rock, paper, scissors game for supernatural creatures, I suspected that vampires would crush witches.

They accepted their coffee quite meekly but both refused a gingersnap.

We all sat back down and Nyx, presumably having been woken by the voices, came padding out of my bedroom and jumped into my lap. I was happy to have her, not only for her warm presence, but for her power.

Gran had taken charge so masterfully it seemed right that

she would continue to lead this very strange coffee party. Looking at Margaret she said, "Now, Margaret Twig, perhaps you can explain to me how a love potion intended to create lasting love has instead caused death."

Go Gran!

Margaret glared at me but didn't dare make my grandmother angry again. "I've no idea. I've made that potion hundreds of times and nothing like this has ever happened. First, it was improperly administered, so people drank it for whom it was not intended. Second, as you know, every magic potion is different. It's not only the ingredients that give it its power but those who make it." Her eyes narrowed on me, increasing the glare and Nyx suddenly stood, arched her back, and hissed at the older witch.

"Good girl," I whispered. The standoff was a brief one.

Margaret Twig uttered a forced laugh and said, "Agnes is right, let's all calm down and work on damage control." She sipped her coffee but I thought she was buying time to choose her words.

She said, "Lucy is, indeed, powerful. But, as we've seen, she can't always control her power. I believe—" she glanced at my grandmother, "—unintentionally, that she imbued the potion with negative energy."

That was so unfair. "But you performed a cleansing spell before we made the potion," I reminded her.

She opened her eyes wide as if to say, well that didn't go so well, did it. I continued, "Anyway, I didn't feel negative. I wanted Alice and Charlie to fall in love. That's all I was thinking about when we were making the potion. I didn't have a single negative thought in my head." Except towards Margaret Twig, but obviously I didn't say that aloud.

Sylvia spoke up, then. She said, "Lucy's just been telling us what happened. There's no actual evidence that that potion was behind the murder."

I was happy to hear those words, and fervently hoped they would turn out to be true. "It could simply be an unfortunate coincidence that while a number of people were under the influence of this spell, a young man was murdered."

Margaret Twig nodded but did not look entirely relieved. "The trouble is that the effects last about three days. Those affected will be spellbound until tomorrow, so they may continue to act irrationally."

I put down my coffee and stood. "I'm going up there. I'm going to talk to every single person who was there last night, and everyone I can find who has anything to do with this play. Someone must've seen or heard something. Ellen Barrymore, the director, is holding an impromptu get together in the theater this evening. Everyone will be there."

"And if you don't find out anything? What then?"

I looked at Margaret steadily. "The police have the wrong man as their prime suspect. Charlie Wright no more killed Jeremy Booth than I did. I will not see an innocent man punished for a crime he didn't commit. If he's arrested, I will tell the police about the potion."

Lavinia gasped and Margaret said, "Lucy, if you do that, you will be expelled from our coven and shunned."

I wasn't surprised. They hadn't come here on a social visit, after all.

I wasn't about to be intimidated by these two and so I kept my voice calm. "I understand. Even though we made the potion at your cottage, with your ingredients, under your supervision, I will not reveal that to the police. I will say that I made the potion myself, here in my kitchen."

Gran exclaimed, "No! Lucy, this isn't your fault."

I was still looking at Lavinia and Margaret. "Yes, it is. I have let myself be pushed into things I wasn't ready for. I had no more business making a love potion than attempting to knit a Scandinavian sweater." I shrugged. "At least if I end up in jail, I'll have plenty of time to improve my knitting skills."

"You won't go to jail," Rafe said, in a confident tone.

"You'll bake me a cake with a file in it?" I asked, my eyebrows raised in fake innocence.

"No. Spirit you out of the country before you're incarcerated."

"But I don't want to be a refugee from justice." I stroked Nyx and immediately felt comforted. "Sylvia, do you believe an actor would murder another actor in order to get their part?"

She wrinkled her nose. "It would depend on the part."

"Seriously?"

She seemed to be thinking harder about the question. "And the venue. No one would kill for a part in the local amdram, but to perform Hamlet or Lady Macbeth in the West End, with a brilliant cast?" She dipped her head back and forth. "That might be worth getting blood on one's hands."

"This is a college production," Lavinia said, sounding scornful.

"That's what I thought," I said. "But Ellen Barrymore is directing it and her next gig is as the artistic director at the Neptune Theatre in London. I'm wondering whether he might have been killed by his understudy."

Sylvia looked unimpressed. "That's a bit obvious, isn't it?"

"Not if someone else gets blamed. Someone like Charlie."

Margaret put down her coffee. "I don't care who killed him, so long as it wasn't caused by that wretched potion."

For once, Margaret and I were in agreement.

Rafe said, "Then there's that missing girl, also one of the troupe of actors. It's too much of a coincidence that two actors could be harmed within a week. They must be connected."

I blew out a breath. "That makes sense, but why? How?"

"I don't know, but I propose to find out."

I was delighted he was going to help, though I'd never doubted he'd end up getting involved. He might be controlling, but he was also good. "Great. Here's what I know. William Matthews says he bumped into Sofia Bazzano after she'd found out she got a tiny part in the production. She was crying. He says he took her to the pub to cheer her up. Police have him on CCTV, in the pub with Sofia. He claims he left her there."

"How much of that story can be corroborated?"

"Ellen Barrymore told the police that she had spoken with Sofia and she was upset." I sighed, feeling like Alice in not wanting Will to have had a hand in Jeremy's death. "And Will is Jeremy's understudy."

"So he gains the most in this death."

"There's one more thing. Jeremy told Scarlett that he had a secret. It seemed to be about his career, but he wouldn't tell her any more."

Rafe nodded. "I'll see if I can find out any more about this missing girl." Then he looked at me. "If Jeremy had a secret, who would he tell?"

I put up my hands. "How would I know?"

"Think, Lucy. If a man is in love with a woman, he wants

to impress her. If Jeremy Booth had something that he thought would make him more desirable, he'd tell the woman. So, who was he infatuated with thanks to that potion?"

My breath drew in on a gasp, all on its own. "Alice!"

CHAPTER 18

*J*umped out of my seat. "I'll call Alice right away and see if Jeremy told her anything about a secret. Then I'm going up to the college." I pretty much repeated what I had said to Alice, that emotions were running high and all the people leaving flowers and tributes for Jeremy were going to have stories and memories to share. Someone was going to let something slip, I was sure of it.

Margaret Twig shrugged. "Well, it's as good a plan as any."

Sylvia reminded me that actors were adept at playing characters quite different than who they really were. "You must see what's behind the mask. If you can, make the mask slip."

Gran and Lavinia both nodded. Only Rafe looked unconvinced. He said, "Before you start provoking actors and pushing their masks around, don't forget that the killer could be there, too. And from behind that mask the murderer will be watching everyone. If Lucy provokes the wrong person, she'll put herself in danger. We can't have that."

Margaret looked at Rafe and then at me and one of her

very irritating knowing smiles curved her lips. She said, "Why don't I put a protection spell on Lucy."

I wasn't falling for that. I said, "Thank you all the same, but I'll cast my own protection spell."

Her eyebrows raised in exaggerated surprise. "You know how to do a protection spell?"

I didn't really, but wasn't about to admit that. With as much dignity as I could muster, I said, "I've been practicing."

Gran, always my greatest fan, said, "Of course, she has. Lucy's an excellent witch. She just needs to be left to go at her own pace."

I grabbed one more gingersnap cookie for the road and then walked up to Cardinal College, for the second time that day, and with a much heavier heart.

On the way, I called Alice's mobile.

I'd worried she'd switch it off while canvassing door to door, but clearly she'd forgotten. She answered right away. "Lucy, is there any news? Is Charlie all right?"

"I imagine so. They're only questioning him, you know. Not torturing a confession out of him." I heard a truck drive by so she must be out on the street. "Have you had any luck?"

"Not yet. Someone thinks they saw the car, but they aren't positive, and they didn't remember anyone being inside."

"Well, keep looking. Someone must have seen him." Then I asked her if Jeremy had said anything to her about exciting news or career prospects.

"In the pub, you mean?"

"Anytime."

"I wasn't really paying that much attention to him in the pub. I was trying to watch Charlie without him realizing. It was obvious he didn't like me talking to Jeremy so I started to feel hopeful."

Poor Jeremy. On his last evening, he'd been hitting on a girl who wasn't even listening. "Do you remember anything?"

"There was one thing. I thought it was a bit odd. He said he was going to be a star, which I thought was idle boasting. Then he looked over at Miles and said, "There's more than one way to the top without stabbing your friends in the back."

"There's more than one way to the top without stabbing your friends in the back? That's what he said?" It was difficult to be certain because it sounded breezy where she was so the sound quality wasn't great.

"Something like that."

"Do you have any idea what Jeremy meant? Did he have an agent or had he gone to auditions? Was Miles going to auditions behind his back?"

"I really don't know. As I said, I wasn't that interested."

Of course, she couldn't have known how important that conversation would be, in retrospect, but I wished she'd listened a bit better. "Okay, thanks. I hope you find someone who remembers Charlie."

"Me, too. At least I'm finally meeting some of my neighbors."

As I continued toward the college I wondered what Jeremy had meant. If Alice had heard him correctly he seemed to have some resentment toward Miles. Miles had insisted it was a friendly rivalry, but maybe they'd been more competitive than friendly. I wondered if they were already auditioning on a professional level. Then I thought about the actual words. He'd talked about being stabbed in the back, and then he'd been hit on the back of the head, and laid down with a sword by his side. It was as close to stabbing someone in the back as the killer could manage without an actual sword.

When I got to the theater wing, there were even more people than I had imagined. This had clearly become the unofficial spot to gather and mourn and, I supposed, for the curious to gossip and ask questions.

As I grew closer I recognized Polly. She looked every inch the tragic heroine as she walked toward where the gathering of flowers and small gifts was growing. She held a single red rose in her hand.

Jeremy wasn't the only victim in this. All the people who had cared for him were also affected. When I caught sight of Polly's face I knew that was no mask. I was looking at real grief.

I was about to walk forward and offer what comfort I could when Scarlett walked across in front of my vision and put her arms around Polly. They cried together for a few minutes and then Scarlett stood while Polly knelt and oh so carefully placed her single rose on the ground.

I looked around at the crying faces, the stunned looking faces, and realized that for most of the students milling around, if they'd ever experienced death it had likely been a grandparent or great grandparent. To lose someone so young, so like them, had put them all in shock. I was pretty shocked, too, but, sadly, I'd had more experience of both death and murder. I was also uncomfortably aware that the murderer was very likely someone associated with this production.

I glanced over to find Miles and Liam and Will standing in a huddle. Miles looked as though he'd been crying. He was smoking a cigarette, something I'd never seen him do, and as he lifted his hand to take a drag, I could see that he was shaking.

Liam looked far too serious for the man who was normally the comedian in the group. Will looked as though he didn't know what to do with his hands. He put them in his pockets, then took them out and rubbed them as though they were cold.

I didn't want Will to turn out to be the murderer, but then I didn't want anyone to turn out to be a murderer. I'd been enjoying the rehearsals and getting to know the actors and crew. I liked these people. However, there was no doubting the fact that the only person I knew who stood to gain from Jeremy's death was Will.

For any of these actors, their big break into show business could be mere weeks away.

There was also the possibility that the murderer didn't even have a classic motive. Perhaps this was someone who liked to kill. Again, my gaze went to Will. He'd been the last person connected to Jeremy to see Sofia. She'd now been missing for five days. I didn't want to take that line of thought any further. It was too horrifying.

I hoped Rafe would find some news of her.

Perhaps a further investigation into Will's background would be a good idea.

Miles saw me and, after hesitating, tossed his cigarette to the ground and walked toward me. I doubted very much that smoking was allowed in this area but it felt like none of the normal rules applied. No doubt, half of these people were meant to be in classes, or studying, but there was a collective urge to band together in grief and shock.

As he came towards me, I saw that all the cockiness was gone. His usual swaggering bravado was nowhere in evidence. I thought of Sylvia telling me to see behind the mask but I didn't need to provoke Miles to see his mask slip. Jeremy's murder had done that. He looked like a vulnerable and frightened boy. His eyes were half wild.

"It's my fault," he said. "If it wasn't for me, Jeremy would still be alive."

He reached into his jacket pocket for a pack of cigarettes and lit another with shaking fingers.

Was he just being dramatic, or was he admitting to murder? I did what Sylvia had suggested. I pushed. "What do you mean?"

He blinked and then those wild eyes focused properly on my face. He shook his head. "Sorry. I don't know what I'm saying. It's just, he was my mate, you know? My wingman. Sure, we jostled for parts, and girls, but it was only for fun."

I felt confused. "Miles, none of that makes you guilty of his death."

A little of the bravado returned and he smirked at me. "That's where you're wrong." He leaned closer to deliver the last line and I smelled the alcohol on his breath.

I was about to suggest he go back to his room and have a nap. But, Sylvia had also reminded me that actors were always playing parts. His role today? Confused and grieving student, feeling that a friendly rivalry somehow implicated him in Jeremy's murder would be very clever if he was actually hiding something much darker.

What if Miles's rivalry with Jeremy had not been quite as friendly as he was maintaining? Jealousy could drive people to desperate acts.

My conversation with Alice was still very much in my mind. Jeremy had said Miles stabbed him in the back. I looked Miles right in the bloodshot eye. "I always sensed there was conflict between you and Jeremy?"

He shook his head, sadly. "My mistress with a monster is in love."

I wanted to stamp my foot. Or slap him. "Stop quoting the play to me. This is serious."

"Serious as the grave."

"What mistress? What monster?"

"Nothing. I'm sorry. I'm not myself."

Before I could probe further, hoping that the alcohol would free his tongue, he said, with a kind of desperation, "Oh God, she can't see me like this." I turned to see what was causing his agitation and Ellen Barrymore had stepped out. She seemed to be looking for someone.

Miles said, "Here," and shoved the burning cigarette at me. I took it instinctively. I'd never smoked and I certainly didn't want to be scolded by the great Ellen Barrymore for smoking outside her theater. No one was looking, so I muttered a spell under my breath that extinguished the cigarette and then tucked it into my pocket before anyone noticed.

The director caught sight of Polly and Scarlett still standing by the flowers. She went up to them and I watched her put an arm around each of the young women.

The three of them looked over at us and then Miles said, urgently, "She can't see me like this. I've been drinking. Tell her I've gone back to my room."

I agreed that I would and he turned to leave.

I kept looking for the thing that didn't fit. The person who should be there and wasn't, the one who was there and shouldn't be, the streak of blood overlooked on a jacket. I didn't even know what I was looking for. But, I became aware that my fingers were tingling and I had a feeling like fingers were stroking my back. I turned around and saw a student walking towards us wearing jeans and a college sweatshirt. Her long hair needed a wash and a comb and her clothes looked like she'd slept in them.

I didn't recognize her from rehearsals, and yet, she was familiar. When she grew closer I gave a gasp. Miles must've heard me for he turned around and cried out the name that was echoing in my head. "Sofia?"

CHAPTER 19

And it was. This was the girl whose face I had seen on posters all over campus and around town. Sofia Bazzano. Only minutes ago I had imagined Will as her murderer, but here she was, looking perfectly healthy.

"Miles!" she said, and her face lit up. She'd been pretty even in a candid shot on a poster but when she looked at Miles her whole face lit up.

He looked so pale I thought he might collapse. I put a hand out but he pulled himself together. He glanced behind him, and then strode forward. In a low, furious, undertone he said, "Get out of here. You've got to leave, now."

As though she couldn't take in his words, she continued walking towards him with her arms held out as though looking for a hug. He stepped back and shook his head. "I'm serious. Go home. I'll call you."

She dropped her arms and looked as though she were about to cry. "I don't understand what's going on." There were dark circles under her eyes and a stain on her sweatshirt that might have been spilled tea. I got the impression that Sofia was usually much better turned out. "Miles?"

He shook his head and stepped back.

I spoke up. "Are you Sofia Bazzano?"

She seemed to drag her gaze away from Miles with difficulty. She looked at me and I could see her searching her memory, trying to place me. I said, "You don't know me. My name is Lucy Swift. Have you seen the police?"

She shook her head, looking miserable. "I didn't know what to do, or where to go. I was on my way back to my room, when I saw Miles."

I understood the urge to bolt for home, but she needed to see the police and soon. "You've been reported as a missing person. There are posters up all over campus, the police are looking for you."

"But I didn't do anything wrong. I think I was kidnapped."

"Did they hurt you?" Miles asked, in an entirely different tone. I heard the caring.

"No. Not really. I don't even know what happened. The last thing I remember, I went to the pub, with Will."

Miles' hands formed fists. "Did he have anything to do with this?"

"I don't know. I don't think so. We were in the pub, and we had a drink, we were both upset about the play. Will had to leave but there was a group of girls I knew from class and so I went to sit with them. I had another pint and then I started feeling really peculiar. I remember going outside to get some fresh air. And that's the last thing I remember until I woke up." She rubbed her head as though mimicking a remembered headache. "I don't know how long had passed, I didn't know where I was, I felt so sick."

"Was anyone else there?" I asked.

"No. I was so frightened. I stood up and discovered I was in a caravan." I immediately translated that in my head to a trailer. "I looked out the window but I was in the middle of a field. My bag was gone, my phone was gone, all I could think of was to get away from there."

"Absolutely," I said. "You were very brave."

She laughed without humor. "I didn't have much choice, did I? I didn't want whoever had done that to me to come back and find me awake. I left the caravan and started walking. But I was weak, and dizzy. I'd found some bottled water in the caravan but there was no food." She screwed up her mouth. "Not that I'd have eaten it. I only took the water because it was sealed. I walked across the fields and I came to a road. I didn't even know which way to go, I chose a direction and started walking. Finally, I came to a village."

"Where was it?" I asked.

"Ainstable." I'd never heard of the town and had no idea where it was, but Miles did.

He said, "Ainstable? That's near Carlisle. Nearly at the Scottish border."

"I know. I don't even know how I got there. I didn't know what to do. I had no money, no phone—"

I was horrified. "You didn't go straight to the police?"

She shook her head. "I was so confused. All I could think about was getting home. I suppose, if there'd been a police station right there I'd have gone in. But I was on a high street in a small town. I went into a village shop and I worked out from the date on the newspaper that I'd been gone for days. I started to tell the shopkeeper my story, hoping she'd at least let me have a sandwich or something. She wasn't sympathetic. I could tell she didn't believe me. I think she thought I was a runaway from school."

"Oh, how awful." I could imagine how frightened and confused she must have been.

"It was. But there was a nice older couple shopping and they bought me a sandwich and a coffee. I think they thought I'd run away from school, too, but they had a granddaughter about my age and they said if she was in trouble they would want someone to help her."

I gave silent thanks to this lovely couple, whoever they were. My heart was pounding just hearing her story.

Miles said, "Why didn't you ask them for some money, or borrow their mobile, so you could phone me, or phone your parents."

"They didn't have a mobile! I told you they were old. And my head was still fuzzy. And I wouldn't call my parents. I don't want them to know about this. They're living in Dubai for my dad's job. They'd only worry."

"No," I said. "They're here. The police got hold of them and they flew in."

She looked really distressed. "They must be so worried."

"Lots of people are worried. Sofia, we need to get you to the police so they can find out who did this."

She was still looking at Miles. "And I did phone you. Last night. I had to take the night train, we got to the station too late for an earlier one. And I borrowed a mobile from a girl I got chatting to. I called you but you didn't pick up."

Miles shifted from one foot to another. "Probably thought it was a marketing call."

"But I left you a message."

"Didn't get it."

"I don't understand what's going on." She rubbed her eyes. "What I really want is a shower and a long sleep in my own bed."

I completely understood how she felt, but I explained how important it was that she tell her story to the police. And, no doubt her parents would want to see for themselves that she was unhurt.

She sighed. "Okay. But I must shower and brush my teeth and change my clothes."

I pulled out my cell phone and called Ian. He picked up, but he sounded brisk and very busy, as he no doubt was with a fresh murder on his hands. Still, at least I had some good news. I told him that Sofia had returned and that she was here, with me.

"Someone will be right over," he said and hung up.

When I told her the police were on their way, her shoulders slumped. She looked at Miles. "Walk me to my room?"

He looked frightened and almost angry. "I can't. Look, I'll call you later." He turned away and then, at the last minute turned back. "So glad you're okay."

She didn't know me at all, but I thought she needed a friend. "I'll walk with you to your room."

I thought she might argue and then she just said, "Thanks." We headed to the dorms.

I'd come back to campus to ask about Jeremy, but now that Sofia was back, I changed tack. If her disappearance was related to Jeremy's death then I wanted to find out what that connection was, and if she was in danger.

"So, after you met the older couple, how did you get here?"

"They drove me to the train station and bought me a ticket." She smiled a little. "I don't think they trusted me. If they'd given me cash, they may have thought I'd do something stupid with it. So, they bought me the ticket and then they bought me some sweets for the ride and a magazine, just as though I had been their granddaughter. I've got their name and address, so I can send them back their money. And I know Mum and Dad will want to thank them."

I wanted to thank them. After all my fears that Sofia had been murdered, it was such a relief to see her back. Of course, people didn't usually knock girls out in bars for no reason. So, as delicately as I could, I asked, "Are you okay, physically?"

"Yes." She shook her head. "I know what you're thinking. But the only voice I heard was a woman's. They didn't interfere with me in any way, if that's what you're worried about."

That was indeed what I was worried about. It was a huge relief. Though, of course, the big question was why? Why would anyone kidnap this nice young woman and abandon her in the middle of nowhere? It made no sense. Could the kidnapping somehow relate to the father's job? Had there been a ransom—demanded and paid—that was kept secret? But that seemed rather far-fetched.

In a day of mysteries, this was one more.

CHAPTER 20

Sofia's dorm room was in one of the old buildings in a quadrangle near the back of the college. I saw now what Theodore had meant when he described the fascinating forest of all different trees that had been planted centuries ago. It must've been an arborist's delight. I was no tree expert, but even I could tell that some of these trees were not the sort to be found in public parks. A lot of them showed their age, with gnarly branches and thick trunks that looked weathered by time and many thousands of students who had sheltered under them, used their trunks for support while studying, probably wooed and cried, debated politics and philosophy and whatever else these brilliant students did.

The lobby of her dorm building wasn't as beautiful as the main buildings on campus. No doubt this had always been a residence. We went up a bare wooden staircase that showed the scars of time. The treads dipped in the middle where countless shoes had trodden up and down. Naturally, there was no elevator.

Her room was on the second floor down a dusty-smelling

corridor. She opened the door and beckoned me inside. It was a typical dorm room. Two beds, two desks, and quite a bit of girlish clutter.

She looked around with fondness, as though she'd imagined she'd never see her home-away-from-home again. "I don't care if I keep the police waiting. I must at least have a shower. And brush my teeth." She shuddered. "And put all these clothes in the wash."

I was somewhat alarmed by her last suggestion. "Sofia, you can't wash them. We'll have to bag them up and give them to the police."

She looked to me as though I was crazy. "My dirty laundry?"

Did this girl spend all her time studying the ancient Greeks or something and never watch modern television shows like CSI? I said, "It's for forensics. You may have picked up a hair from your kidnapper or something." I didn't really know either, but just in case there was evidence to be had off her clothing, I wasn't about to stand by while she threw it in the laundry.

She looked irritated by my suggestion but rolled her eyes and said, "Fine. See if you can find a bag in my desk there." And then she grabbed her shower kit and a blue bath towel.

Even if she hadn't told me which side of the room was hers, I'd have worked it out. On top of her desk was a photograph of her and Miles with their arms around each other, grinning. I went towards it. "Are you and Miles seeing each other?"

She suddenly swung around and, in true entitled rich girl fashion said, "Who are you, again?"

I accepted that she was stressed and worn out from being

kidnapped, but still, that seemed like a lot of attitude towards a stranger who was only trying to help her. I said, at my gentlest, "I'm Lucy Swift. I'm a community volunteer, helping out with A Midsummer Night's Dream."

Her tired eyes looked suspicious. "Are you sure you're not more interested in Miles Thompson than in Shakespeare?"

I was so stunned I blinked. Then I realized how this might look to her. I shook my head. "No. Miles is a great guy, but, believe me, I'm not interested in him." I let out a breath. "I didn't want to be the one to tell you, but you should know everything that's been going on around here."

She looked skeptical. "You mean something more dramatic than me being kidnapped?"

"I'm afraid so. Jeremy Booth Is dead."

She dropped her washing kit and it hit the ground with a plop. I don't think she noticed. "Jeremy? Dead? But that's impossible. He's so young, so full of life."

I didn't say anything. She'd already had a traumatic experience so I let her absorb my words at her own pace. She looked at me as though I might be joking but when I clearly wasn't she said, in a milder tone, "When? What happened?"

"It happened some time in the night or early this morning. He was murdered."

Her eyes opened wide and she took a step back as though just the word murder was dangerous. As though I, the deliverer of the word, might be dangerous. "Murdered?"

I nodded. "Now you see how important it is for you to tell the police everything about your own recent experience."

She backed up another step and her hip hit the doorway. "You mean I was going to be murdered?" Her voice rose to a shrill pitch on the last word.

"No. That's not what I'm saying. There may be no connection at all. But you have to admit it's odd that you get mysteriously kidnapped and Jeremy gets killed all within a few days."

She put her hands over her face then and moaned, "Oh, poor Jeremy."

"Can you think of anyone who might want to hurt him?"

"No. Of course not. He's lovely."

"Is there any connection between the two of you? Something that might explain your kidnapping and his murder?" I couldn't help but recall Miles's strange behavior when she'd turned up. Was there some kind of love triangle going on? If she and Jeremy had become close, could Miles have decided to end their relationship in a brutal fashion?

I watched her carefully, hoping that in her vulnerable state she'd be more likely to talk about things she might normally keep to herself, but she looked genuinely mystified. "What connection could there possibly be? We share one class and both belong to the theater troupe. Where he's a lead and I am basically stage decoration." She rubbed her forehead. "My head hurts. I can't even think straight."

I picked up her kit bag and handed it to her. "Go and get that shower now. It will make you feel better."

She took a dressing gown off a hook behind the door and left and I breathed out. Slowly. And back in again.

I tried to center myself inside her room. I was glad to have it to myself as well as permission to look inside her desk. It made my sleuthing so much easier. First, I looked around. I closed my eyes and called on my witch powers. I felt a clutter of emotions: anxiety, elation, anger, triumph, envy. However, with two women sharing the room and who knew how many people coming through here, it was impossible to tell which were Sofia's emotions. What I hadn't felt was the darkness of evil.

Whoever, or whatever had stolen her away, they hadn't been in this room.

She had told me to look into her desk for a bag to put her discarded clothing into, so I didn't feel quite so much that I was snooping, though I must admit, my eyes searched for more than just a bag. I didn't even know what I was looking for, some sort of clue to activities, acquaintances, something that might have provoked a kidnapping.

Despite her earlier assertion that she and Jeremy were only friends, I searched for any connection between her and the murdered actor. She hadn't admitted that she was seeing Miles but from her reaction to my question, and the photo on her desk, it seemed clear that she had been. Miles, not Jeremy.

In her desk drawer was a handful of snapshots that someone had printed. I flipped through them rapidly. There were Miles and she with their arms around each other, against a river with swans floating by. Another of her and Polly and Jeremy, and another of the four of them plus Will, who stood with one arm slung around Sofia's shoulders on one side, and his other around Scarlett. I recognized the background. They were at Stratford-on-Avon.

Will. He'd been the last of the theater people to see Sofia, and he was the one who would step into Jeremy's role. But there was also Miles, who'd been acting so very peculiar today. He'd been friends and supposedly friendly rivals with Jeremy and, obviously, romantically involved with Sofia. But why on earth would he kidnap her? Or have her kidnapped? It made no sense.

I was still rooting through her desk when the door opened. I couldn't believe it. No one with hair that long could shower so quickly, especially someone who hadn't been near water or soap for several days.

I turned and saw an older couple, probably in their forties, complete strangers to me. As I was to them.

They looked attractive, rich, and, from the pale skins and dark circles, I would say they were both sleep deprived. "Who are you?" asked the woman, instantly suspicious. "And where's Sofia?"

She looked as though she might burst into tears finding me in this room. It didn't take a detective or a genius to work out that these must be Sofia's parents. I rose and smiled. "Sofia's fine. She's just taking a shower. You're her parents, I presume?"

The woman calmed down at my words. "Yes. Are you a police officer?"

"No. I'm a friend." Stretching the definition of friend, but I was certainly not an enemy and I was very pleased that Sofia had come back. Not nearly as pleased as her parents were.

Her mother walked to one of the beds and sat down on it. "I won't relax until I see her for myself."

The father went and sat beside her and took her hand. "Neither will I." He turned to me. "Do you know what happened to her?"

"She'll tell you herself. She believes she was kidnapped."

He looked shocked and horrified, as well he might. "Kidnapped? Whatever for?"

"I don't know. I wondered whether you'd been contacted for ransom. Or whether you have the kind of job that..." My words petered out. Everything I knew about kidnapping and ransom I'd learned from television.

He shook his head before I'd even finished. "I don't have that kind of job. Not important enough. And we're certainly not rich enough. If someone wanted ransom, there are a lot of students here that would be riper pigeons to pluck." His face went ruddy. "She's so young and beautiful. She wasn't—hurt in anyway?"

"She says not."

His eyes closed and he breathed out a sigh of relief.

When Sofia arrived back from the shower, her long dark hair in wet ringlets around her shoulders, wearing her dressing gown and carrying the clothes she'd been kidnapped in, she took one look at her parents and threw herself into her mother's arms. "Mummy, Daddy, I'm so glad you're here. It was so awful."

Both the women burst into tears and her father rubbed her back awkwardly. He said, "We've got a car, love. We're taking you straight to the police."

"Did DI Chisholm call you?" I asked. I didn't want to interrupt this reunion, but Ian had said he was sending someone to talk to Sofia.

Dad shook his head. "Didn't have to. We were there. I told him we'd come and get her and take her back to the police station." Then he said to Sofia, "We will find out who did this to you." He said again, menace in his voice, "We will."

Not wanting to intrude any longer, I packed her discarded clothes into a cloth bag I'd found and asked Sofia's father to make sure that Ian got the bag of clothes in order to test for forensic evidence. He nodded and thanked me briefly and then I made my escape.

My brain was spinning. Could there be a connection between Sofia's bizarre kidnapping and Jeremy's equally bizarre murder? On the one hand it seemed so unlikely, but, given the timing, how could they not be related?

The next person I needed to see was Will.

I walked back across the quad to the theater. A few new flower attributes had been laid. There were, however, fewer people standing outside now. I wasn't certain if they had dispersed or simply gone inside either because it was warmer or in some strange compulsion to be near where the disaster had happened, perhaps to watch the police at work.

I walked into the theater building and found most people had moved back inside.

Small groups stood, sniffling and chatting, but the sense of anxiety was like a cold chill that had entered. People stood huddled into themselves, and closer to those they were talking to, as though they could share body heat and perhaps remain safer.

I scanned the crowd and spotted Miles and Will standing together. I was about to walk over when a kind of flutter went through the gathered students. I looked up to see a uniformed police officer coming from the direction of the theater, holding a plastic evidence bag.

Inside, was a script.

As the police officer walked by, Scarlett looked at the script in the evidence bag and then glanced up. She said, "Miles? Isn't that your script?"

He shook his head. "Couldn't be. My script's in my bag."

She looked as though she was going to argue with him and then seemed to change her mind. She turned her back and began to speak to Polly in a low voice. I remembered seeing Miles with his script last night, at the pub, but they all looked alike. The actors tore various scenes out of their binders to keep rehearsals simple, so there wasn't a front page with the actor's name scribbled across the front.

A whisper travelled down the wide corridor, like a puff of breeze through a wheat field. It was information being passed from group to group. I heard Daffyd, the boy who was playing Bottom the Weaver turn to Liam, who was behind him, and say, "They found that script on the stage. Near Jeremy's body. What do you reckon? It belongs to the murderer?"

I glanced at Miles and I thought that everyone who had heard Scarlett's words must be looking at him, too. He looked pale and shaken. He muttered something and then walked out the doors into the cold. He didn't have his backpack with him.

Scarlett saw me and came over. "Lucy, I'm sure that was Miles's script. I recognized it. He'd torn a corner of the front page off to make a note. They're saying the script was left on the stage. Where Jeremy was—"

I was still looking through the glass upper part of the doors where Miles was stalking away. His hands were shoved in his pockets, the line of his back rigid.

She asked, "Why would he lie about where his script was?"

Miles was headed towards the accommodation blocks. No doubt he was going to rifle through his schoolbag to see if he could find his script. I said, "Maybe he left it on the stage by accident. It could've fallen out of his bag without him noticing."

Her eyes widened in shock. "But, he had the script at the

pub last night. You remember. He and Liam were messing about pretending to do the scene in Welsh."

I nodded. I remembered it well. It had been hilarious at the time. Now, it didn't seem so funny.

"If Miles left it on the stage, that means—"

I didn't answer. There was no point finishing that sentence, she could work out the end of it for herself.

Miles? Killing Jeremy? Why?

And why had he acted so peculiar around Sofia?

CHAPTER 21

*A*bout four o'clock, Ellen Barrymore invited everyone to come into the large rehearsal hall. Those who had hoped for a glimpse of the murder scene would be disappointed as it was still cordoned off by police. Meeting in the main theater would've been a macabre choice anyway, especially for Scarlett and Ellen and me. It was bad enough going into the rehearsal hall where I remembered so well Jeremy and Miles fooling around on that first day, drinking that love potion and throwing it in the coffee urn with no idea of the chaos they were about to cause.

Jeremy had been gorgeous, full of life, and exactly the kind of young actor destined to rise rapidly in his career and end up as a household name. To think of him, murdered, before he'd properly begun, seemed so cruel.

The sadness pressed on all of us as we entered that big room. The same room where we had gathered with such enthusiasm only a couple of days ago, ready to work together to create a comic masterpiece. Now we were bathed in tragedy.

I looked around and, to my surprise, saw Rafe walk in the door and head towards me. I couldn't believe he'd waltzed in here as though he owned the place. "What are you doing here? You've nothing to do with the play."

"Very astute of you," he said in that snooty, superior tone of his. "In fact, I have some news I think you'll find interesting."

I was trying to keep a low profile, do some snooping and trying to get a killer's mask to slip. Having a tall, dark and gorgeous vampire by my side was not going to help me keep a low profile. Already, I could feel the buzz of interest he created.

"Can you tell me later?" I asked in a low, urgent voice. "Back at my flat? Ellen specifically said we were to keep this meeting to cast and crew."

I felt a prickle of foreboding between my shoulder blades. I glanced behind me and turned back to Rafe, in horror. "Oh no, here she comes. You'd better leave."

Instead of doing as I asked, and when did he ever? Rafe turned toward Ellen and extended his hand. What was he, a groupie looking for an autograph? I was trying to think up some excuse as to why he might be here, and to assure Ellen that he was leaving immediately, when I saw her smile at Rafe and clasp his hand.

"Rafe. How lovely of you to join us. I'm so sorry that it's under such tragic circumstances."

"I'm sorry too, Ellen. From what I've been hearing, Jeremy Booth was a remarkable young actor."

Her eyes filled with sudden tears. She blinked them away. "He was. One of my brightest. He had such a career in front of him, I can hardly bear to think of it." She brought her other hand to cover their still-clasped ones. "I must circulate and talk to the students. Thank you for coming. Your support means the world to me, especially now."

As she walked away Rafe turned back to me. "I'm sorry, you were saying?"

"Oh, knock it off," I said irritably. "I might've known you two would be bosom buddies." I put on a fake swooning British accent. "Oh, Rafe, your support means the world to me."

His lips twitched in reluctant amusement. "You've missed your calling. You should be on the stage, not helping behind the scenes."

"Not likely. Anyway, what did you find out?"

He glanced around and then dropped his voice. "I took a look through the surveillance footage at the pub where Sofia had her last drink."

I was confused and I'm sure my face showed that. "But, the police have already been through that footage. That's how they discovered the photo of William Matthews." I indicated with a motion of my chin where Will was standing with Liam and Daffyd.

"Yes, they did. And, after they found footage of William Matthews they stopped looking any further. I have more time than most coppers do." He said it with a kind of deadpan irony since, as we both knew, he had all the time in the world, quite literally.

"There was a woman who came in, by herself, about half an hour after Sofia and Will arrived. She wouldn't have been remarkable except that she was standing at the bar when

Sofia's second pint was poured. The footage is fuzzy, of course, but you can see her leaning her hand out to get the bartender's attention just as Sofia's pint is served up."

"You mean, she could've been the one to slip some kind of drug into the drink?"

"Exactly."

I felt excitement beat behind my breastbone. "Sofia said she remembered hearing a woman's voice. She'd have to be strong enough to carry an unconscious student."

"Yes. I only saw her back and part of her side. She wore a cap, probably deliberately, and there are no good shots of her face. But she was hefty. Solid."

"What was she wearing?"

"Looked like jeans, and some kind of dark jacket. Unremarkable. She had a set of keys hanging from her back pocket, like a tradesman."

"Maybe the police can get more from that footage. Or connect a stocky female with a vehicle. Maybe a tradesman's van? Suitable for transporting unconscious women without being spotted."

"Perhaps."

Scarlett came running up. "Lucy, I didn't see you before. I'm so glad you're here." I'd become used to seeing that look in her eyes when she gazed at me, but it was becoming tiresome. I knew she was under the influence of that potion, but I had a murder to solve.

When Polly beckoned her over, she huffed out a breath and rolled her eyes. "She's so needy. I'll be right back."

I turned to Rafe. "Tomorrow cannot come soon enough."

He looked amused. "What happens tomorrow?"

"This potion should finally wear off. Unless Margaret Twig's been lying to me again."

He shook his head and looked down at me in that odiously condescending way he had. "Lucy, when are you going to step into your power?"

"Step into my power? Who are you? Tony Robbins?"

"Tony who?"

I tended to forget that Rafe was not one to keep up with modern culture. "Never mind. What's all this about stepping into my power?"

"You shouldn't need me to tell you. I'm not even a wizard, but I know you're a very powerful witch. You can end the spell anytime."

If he'd hit me up the side of the head with the lid of a trash can I couldn't have been more shocked. "I can?"

His cashmere-clad shoulders rose up and down once. "I don't see why not. You helped make the potion and, I suspect, part of the reason Margaret Twig is so wary of you is that she senses your power is greater than hers."

This was the best news I'd had in a very dark day. "Really?"

"I believe so."

"Sweet."

He said, "I think I'll wander around and eavesdrop. Perhaps I'll learn something useful. Good luck."

"You too." He had the keenest hearing of anyone I knew, so if anyone dropped a clue, Rafe would be there to catch it. Assuming, of course, that he could translate modern, student slang.

I was mildly suspicious that he'd shown up to keep an eye

on me. Overbearing he might be, but he was protective as well and, when he wasn't driving me crazy, I liked knowing that he had my back.

Alice and Theodore came in and I could tell from Alice's expression that they hadn't found anyone who could confirm that Charlie spent the night outside her house. That was disappointing. As though she felt my gaze, she turned her head and when she spotted me in the crowd shook her head slightly.

I'd have gone over but the student playing Titania went running over to her. My hearing wasn't as good as Rafe's but it was better than most. I heard her say, "Oh, Alice, I heard they arrested Charlie. It's such a shock."

Drama queen. Alice patiently explained that Charlie hadn't been arrested as he was innocent. Then I couldn't hear anymore as another voice intruded.

"Oh, look, Theodore's here," a female voice cried out in delight and the two scene painters who were vying for his affections elbowed past each other trying to reach him.

Alice's new friend lost interest when Alice refused to share her horror about Charlie's arrest.

Alice walked over to Jeremy's photograph and was paying her respects, when I saw Charlie come in. He looked tired and a bit pugnacious. I could tell he hadn't had a very happy time being interviewed. Ian had obviously played bad cop/bad cop. He was scanning the room, no doubt looking for Alice. He was waylaid by the woman playing Hippolyta, who looked as though she'd run off with him if he'd only say the word.

I looked around the room. I ought to be trying to spot suspicious behavior, but all I saw was evidence of mismatched lovers. The two scene painters were both flirting with Theodore so hard their lips must hurt from all that smiling and sweet words. He looked tormented, though I thought mildly flattered as well.

Still, I had had enough. I could feel the chaos of lovelorn feelings, confusion and betrayal all around me. This had to stop.

Was Rafe correct? Did I have enough power to override the love potion? I wished he'd told me that two days ago. It would have saved a lot of embarrassment and heartache. Charlie was obviously over his infatuation with Polly, so clearly the three-day effect wasn't absolute. I wondered if the potion wore off at different times for different people depending, perhaps, on how much they'd drunk, or whether their feelings were already engaged. When this was over, I would have to ask Gran or Lavinia. Margaret as a last resort.

I could only try to break the spell. If I failed, we'd be no worse off. If I succeeded, I'd begin to wonder whether Rafe might be right and my power, once I learned to control it, was stronger than Margaret's.

I spent about a minute imagining all the things I could turn her into. I had a sneaking suspicion that she could turn herself into a cat at will. Something about her face and movements were uncannily cat-like. Anyway, turning her into a cat was too good for her. It might be fun to turn her into a mouse, though, and let Nyx play with her. I enjoyed that fantasy for several seconds. However, Nyx being a familiar probably wouldn't play along. I wanted her to terrorize Margaret, not treat her like an equal.

In A Midsummer Night's Dream, Bottom the Weaver is given a donkey's head and Titania, queen of the fairies, falls in love with him through some trickery. That could be fun. Seeing a very proud witch in love with someone not anywhere near her equal.

I gasped out loud. It was as though I'd turned a kaleidoscope one extra turn and had a completely different picture in front of me.

"Lucy, Polly's being such a pain. Let's get out of here. It's too depressing. We should go dancing. I know a great club."

"Scarlett," I snapped. "You don't love me. You're under a spell."

Her lips curved. "I know. And I hope I never wake up. I know you feel the same way. I can see it in your eyes."

"No. You're seeing what you want to see. Your eyes are blinded by a kind of love-madness."

"No. I've never felt this way before. You have to love me. You have to." I thought she was going to cry.

Anything was better than this. If I accidentally turned all the cast and crew of A Midsummer Night's Dream into field mice, or made them all suddenly turn away from love altogether, I was sorry, but I had to clear the air. I couldn't think with all the confused emotions clogging my senses.

"I'd do anything for you," Scarlett exclaimed.

"Go and ask Miles to come over here."

She began to pout. "What do you want him for?"

"I need his help."

She looked disappointed but wandered off to look for him.

Ellen had made her way around the rehearsal hall, very much like a cocktail party hostess working the room, and I sensed she was getting ready to begin this impromptu memorial.

I heard a commotion at the door, cries of, "It can't be. Sofia?" And turned to see the student who'd been lost, welcomed back into the fold.

Even though she still looked tired, she'd styled her hair, put on makeup and was dressed in clean clothes. She looked gorgeous.

I heard the buzz of voices as more people received the news and went to see for themselves that Sofia had returned, unharmed.

Ian had come in with her. I saw him look over the room. He nodded briefly when he saw me but his eyes kept moving. I knew the minute he spotted Scarlett for an utterly fatuous expression crossed his face and he started towards her.

"Enough." I said aloud.

"I quite agree," said a blonde woman standing beside me, who I thought was something to do with costumes. She nodded as though I'd said something profound, then took a nip from a flask.

I didn't have my grimoire with me. I didn't have a potion that anyone could drink as an antidote to the first one. Even if I had, I wouldn't have dared let these already spell-bound mortals drink another potion I'd brewed. I did, however, have power.

Sometimes my power sent ancient standing stones flying through the air, by accident, and blew up my kitchen, again by accident, but sometimes, I got it right.

I believed that if I could focus, I could make this work.

I remembered the words I'd said over the first potion. I thought I might be able to reverse the spell by making up a rhyme of my own. I wasn't sure if it was the actual words that mattered or the way they centered the witch's intent, though I suspected the latter.

All I needed was a little space.

And fire. The words arrived in my head, and the second I received them, I knew that was right. We'd made the spell with water, fire was its opposite. The words sounded like they were spoken, but in my head, though I heard the slight lilt of an Irish accent.

But where was I going to get fire from? I looked over at Jeremy's memorial corner, as though my gaze was being pulled there and saw Liam had a trio of stubby beeswax candles that he was pulling from his backpack.

Perfect.

I walked forward, arriving as he'd lit the last wick. The candles glowed deep gold and the smell of honey began to waft into the air.

I took a deep breath.

"Lucy," Scarlett's voice interrupted me. "I couldn't find Miles. I tried. Come on, let's—"

"Scarlett, just the woman I want," Liam said, and before she could reach me, he'd taken her arm and was leading her away.

He turned and, looking at me over her shoulder, winked.

I nodded to him, acknowledging his help and our secret kinship. I knew that he'd keep my sacred space clear for the minute or two I needed.

Once more, I centered myself. I imagined all these confused relationships as a piece of knitting I'd tangled. I pictured the knots unwinding, the snarls straightening and the comfort of a perfect piece of knitting. Then, looking into the flame of the tallest and brightest of the three candles, I said:

THIS LOVE POTION's work is over and done
  Remove the love blindness from everyone
  The truth of their hearts let them see
  So I say, so mote it be

The words were as simple as a child's rhyme, but when I said the last words, the candle flared and its flame rose high, while the two smaller candles followed suit, the three flames rising into the air and receding like a fountain.

I turned and, all at once, I felt the crazed emotions begin to calm.

The two women making fools of themselves over Theodore, shook their heads and settled down. Scarlett looked at me as though, for a second, she couldn't quite place me. Then she turned and looked around as though she'd lost something very precious.

Polly was standing, not far away, watching her, and when their gazes connected, I said, "Ah." Soon they were together, laughing.

The woman playing Hippolyta found the guy playing Theseus and they began to flirt. Good. Things were settling. Now I could think.

Liam was standing looking at Scarlett and Polly when I came up beside him. "Thanks for the help."

"Anytime."

"Liam, when you saw Charlie climb over the wall last night, what time was it?"

"Exactly?"

"Yes."

He screwed up his face, remembering. "Well, I was at the pub for last call, that's eleven. I was chatting to a girl, and we talked for a bit outside, so probably I was back at the college a bit before midnight. I saw Charlie climb over the wall to get in about five past twelve, I suppose. And then I went up to my room. I looked out my window, I suppose I was a bit worried about what he was up to. He climbed back over the wall only a few minutes later. About quarter past twelve."

"Thanks."

"I don't want to chuck him in it. He seems a nice guy. But so was Jeremy."

"You're doing the right thing. Tell me, how do you get in when it's late?" I'd always arrived when the Porter's Lodge was open, but I didn't think they sat there all night letting students come and go.

"There's a key pad set into the gate. They like us to be in before eleven, but it's not like the old days, when there was a curfew."

"So, students can get in, but presumably no one else would have the code?"

"That's right. And there are cameras, of course, recording who comes and goes. Plus, we have security guards on premises at night."

Ellen was making her way to the stage, where a microphone had been set up. I said to Liam, "I need you to do something for me. Stand at the entrance to the rehearsal hall and don't let anyone leave."

His green eyes narrowed on my face. "Happy to do it, but why?"

"I have an idea that might shake some clues loose."

His eyebrows rose. "Do you know who killed Jeremy?"

"I'm almost certain I do. I'm hoping to provoke a confession."

He looked skeptical. "You think the killer's going to confess?"

"No. Someone else is."

His skepticism turned to concern. "You watch yourself. This killer isn't afraid to bash people's heads in." He glanced significantly at Jeremy's photo behind my head.

"I know. I'll be careful."

"Blessed be," he said softly, before heading for the door.

Rafe came over to my side. "Nicely done. The effects of the love potion are no more and the scales have fallen from the eyes of the love-blind."

"I know," I said, still feeling pleased with myself.

"Perhaps you'll have more faith in your own skills in the future."

"Perhaps, I will."

He looked at me, amusement mixed with wariness in the depth of his ice blue eyes. "You're pleased about more than your spell reversal. You're plotting something."

"Yes. And I need your help."

"Naturally."

I shook my head at him. "Any man with a modicum of charm and address will do, so if you're going to be sarcastic, I'll find another helper."

"I'm yours to command."

"I need you to keep Miles within your sight, and preferably your reach."

His brows rose, but he nodded in agreement. "And while I'm doing that, what will you be doing?"

"Nothing dangerous. I'll be giving a little tribute to Jeremy. That's all."

"Don't do anything foolish."

"If I do, you'll be here to protect me."

I said it flippantly, but he answered seriously. "Always."

CHAPTER 22

*T*wo stage hands came over and asked us to move out of the way so they could take Jeremy's picture up onto the stage.

Knowing I didn't have much time, I went over to Charlie, who was standing hand-in-hand with Alice and asked him about his late night visit to Cardinal College the night before. I was relieved that his answer tallied with my guess.

Once the stagehands had placed Jeremy's photograph on its easel up on stage, and taken the candles up as well, obviously thinking they were part of the memorial, Ellen walked up and stood in front of the microphone.

It was exactly like the first day we'd all met here. Even Alex Blumstein was at the back of the room as she had been on the first day, looking like a bouncer. Liam stood beside her. He seemed to be making small talk, though I could see he was doing all the talking. Bless him.

Rafe had found Miles, who was standing, alone, and leaning a shoulder against the wall. His eyes were swollen and he looked as though he'd met Tragedy for the first time in his life and she'd kicked his butt.

Alex Blumstein dimmed the lights, so Ellen was spotlighted on the stage, and so was Jeremy's photograph. She began speaking in her beautiful voice. "Thank you all for coming." She paused, looked over at Jeremy's photo and shook her head. "I would give anything not to be here at this moment on this tragic day."

She pressed her lips together as though fighting for control. When she spoke again, I could hear the suppressed tears.

"Jeremy Booth was a fine actor, as so many of you know. But he was more than that. He was a friend, an excellent student and a fine rower, having been on the men's eight that won a gold medal this year at the World University Rowing Championships in China."

There was a smattering of applause.

"I first met Jeremy when he auditioned for me nearly a year ago." She smiled as though the memory were bittersweet. "Jeremy chose a scene from Hamlet. It was an audacious choice and showed a self-confidence and assurance that appealed to me in one so young. His confidence inspired others, too. He was always willing to work hard, to help others become better and, added to all that he had an extremely good sense of humor. As we all know, he loved a good laugh."

There were murmurs of agreement.

"As the shock of this tragedy begins to sink in, I wanted us to meet here together on this very sad day. Later, there will be a funeral, memorials and celebrations of his life. But here, this evening, I wanted us—his theater family—to gather together, not only to remember Jeremy, but to remember also that we always have each other. I will do anything to make sure that we can stay together."

Her gaze had been roving over the audience but at the last words she glanced over at Miles. In that moment he looked so murderous that a chill went down my spine.

"I know everyone here has memories of Jeremy, no doubt a funny story or two. I invite anyone who is so moved to come up here and share a little about *their* Jeremy Booth." She put out a hand in general invitation and then stepped back, out of the limelight.

She needn't have worried that there'd be no takers. In a room full of budding actors there was very soon a line of people who wanted to say a few words. Scarlett among them. I was surprised that she wanted to go up there, having made the grisly discovery, but perhaps talking about him would help her process the shock.

Before the line grew too long I eased forward and took my place behind Daffyd.

The first speaker had been to prep school with Jeremy and told an amusing story about a prank the two of them had played, when Jeremy had pretended to be the nurse coming into the dorm to dose them all for lice. "He was always a good mimic. We laughed for weeks after." He looked at the grinning man in the photo. "I'll miss you, mate."

Then Scarlett took her turn. She looked out over the group and took a dramatic pause, something she'd no doubt learned from Ellen Barrymore. "I was to play Hermia. In the play, Hermia loves Lysander, played by Miles Thompson over there. For some reason, Demetrius also falls in love with her. Demetrius, of course, would have been played by Jeremy. In the play, Hermia never once has soft feelings for Demetrius. You can tell, he's just getting on her nerves, always after her, telling her how beautiful she is and how much he loves her. But, real life is not really like a play, is it?"

She looked out on the audience and from where I stood, looking up, I could see her eyes glistening with tears. She blinked them away. "I did love Jeremy Booth. I loved his playfulness and the way he could always make me laugh, even on a bad day. I loved how clever he was and how much he tried to hide it from the rest of us. When he put his mind to something he was fiercely determined. Anyone who ever watched him during a rowing regatta knows exactly what I mean."

There were murmurs of appreciation, a couple of whistles, and some clapping.

"Great things were going to happen for Jeremy. And the wonderful thing about him was, he knew it. He had so much confidence—he believed he would do whatever he set his mind to. I'm always so insecure and worried about screwing it all up and getting things wrong, but he just went straight forward and didn't let anything get in this way. If I can learn anything from Jeremy, it's to live my life with that kind of focus. And so, Jeremy—" here she turned to gaze at his photograph and that eternally grinning face, "—please know that when I gave you the cold shoulder in the play, I was only pretending. I really did love you." Her voice became suspended with tears. "I don't know when we'll meet again, but until we do, the stage will be an emptier place without you."

Several people wiped their eyes, and I could hear a few noses blowing, as Daffyd got up. He told a story about how he'd been put in an improvisation scene with Jeremy. "It was an interrogation scene. I was a prisoner and he was interrogating me. I had to remain completely serious. He started asking me name, rank, and serial number, and then he started asking about marmalade. Like, did I know where marmalade came from?"

Daffyd had a naturally comic way about him, so when he looked out at the audience, and rolled his eyes, everyone laughed.

"He'd bark out these questions in this angry voice and the whole scene was about *marmalade*. Where was I hiding the marmalades?" He laughed then, in memory. "The more I tried to play it straight, the crazier his questions got. He asked, 'What about the thick bits? Was there a secret factory where they made the thick pieces?'" He shook his head. "I learned as much in that scene about comedy as I probably learned in any class." He turned here and looked back, "No offense, Ellen."

He ended with a short prayer in Welsh. As the beautiful words rolled over us, I didn't think there was a dry eye in the room.

It was my turn next.

My shoes made clomping noises that seemed to echo. Ellen was standing just out of the circle of light and she nodded at me when I took my place. I looked out over the room, making certain that Liam was in place, which he was, and that Rafe was standing very near to Miles, which he also was.

Everyone was looking at me, waiting.

"I didn't know Jeremy Booth very well. In fact, I only met him a few days ago, at the beginning of rehearsals. However, after hearing the previous tributes and from my own experience I know that Jeremy Booth was full of talent and would've gone places if he hadn't been murdered here, today."

I felt a shudder of horror go through the room. Even though everyone knew he'd been murdered, it was still a shock to hear the word. "We cannot bring him back, though I wish we could. But we can, together, help solve his murder and make sure the culprit is punished."

From the corner of my eye I saw Ellen walking towards me looking stern. "Thank you very much," she said in that clear voice that would carry to the back of the stalls. "We'll let the police do that job."

She intended to take back control of the microphone, but I had anticipated that and grabbed the mic off the stand. I turned my back to her so she would have to physically wrench the microphone away from me if she wanted it back.

I said, "I know who killed Jeremy."

I let the gasps of shock and horror bubble through the crowd. "And I can prove it, with your help."

"Lucy!" Ellen Barrymore demanded. "Stop this. Someone, help me."

We must have looked like we were acting out a crazy improv scene from down on the floor. She was reaching around me and trying to grab the mic, and I was pushing her off. Then she ran around in front of me and I turned my back on her. She looked to the back where Alex Blumstein stood. "Alex! Cut the power to the mic."

But Liam was still standing beside Alex and he called from the very back. "I want to hear what Lucy has to say. Who else does?"

A lot of people yelled out that they wanted me to continue.

Ellen was red in the face and vibrating with fury. "I will not have this. You're interfering in a police investigation."

I looked out. It was difficult to make out individual faces so I called, "Detective Inspector Ian Chisholm? Do I have your permission to continue?"

I wasn't sure whether he'd let me, since my sleuthing, like my dramatic ability, was amateur at best, but he replied, in his clear, commanding tone, "I'd also like to hear what Lucy has to say."

"Well I wouldn't," Ellen shouted. "This is meant to be a dignified sendoff for a beloved member of our cast. I will not see it turned into an amateur farce." She stomped off the stage and down the stairs and headed for the exit.

Liam stepped quietly into the middle of the doorway and I said into the microphone, "Please, don't leave, Ms. Barrymore. There are some questions that only you can answer."

She turned back towards me and threw up her hands. "This is intolerable. I will not stay while some knitting shop owner with delusions that she's Miss Marple makes a fool of all of us."

Ian obviously had no idea what I was doing, but he knew I wouldn't put on this public performance without a reason. My problem was, I had no proof, only a theory that I knew to the tips of my tingling fingers was right. I had to provoke the right people to the right actions.

Ian strode across the rehearsal hall to intercept Ellen Barrymore. He said, loud enough that most of us could hear him, "Please stay."

She drew herself up to her full height. "Is that an order?"

"If you want to phrase it like that, yes."

"I will be calling my lawyer."

"Of course. As soon as we're finished here, you can call anyone you like."

With a sound of fury, she turned and crossed her hands in front of her breasts and glared at me.

I felt the intense gazes of everyone in the room on me and hoped, quite fervently, not only that I was correct, but that I didn't mess up the investigation. I looked at Liam and he nodded, reassuringly. I glanced at Rafe and for once that tickle of coolness was like a refreshing shower over my over-heated skin. I drew in a deep breath and centered myself. I had to be very careful to lay facts out in the correct order.

It was like building a house of cards. If I fumbled, the whole thing would come crashing down and instead of solving a murder I'd be playing Fifty-Two Pick Up with my reputation.

I took a breath and spoke once more into the mic. "A Midsummer Night's Dream was an excellent choice for these young actors. It's about the way we manipulate people in the name of love, when sometimes what we really crave is power."

I let that sink in for a moment. "I'm neither a scholar nor an actor but I've been listening to the conversations around this play. It opens with Theseus and Hippolyta about to be married. But Hippolyta's a captive and a slave. She seems to be resigned to her fate but make no mistake, this woman has no choice." I cringed inside as I heard myself, with my junior college English, lecturing some of the brightest scholars in the world and people who knew Shakespeare a lot better than I did. No one was laughing, though, so I continued.

"Then there are the young lovers. Hermia, played by Scar-lett Baker, Lysander, played by Miles Thompson, Helena played by Polly Johnson and Demetrius, played by Jeremy Booth. They are also manipulated and not always acting with free will. Even poor Bottom the Weaver is turned into a donkey for sport and then, in another romantic manipulation, the king of the fairies causes the queen of the fairies to fall in love with that donkey, again using his power to manipulate."

I was starting to sound like SparkNotes. I needed to move this along. "Ellen Barrymore has a policy, that all of you know, and that I've heard about from several sources. She doesn't allow her actors to date each other during production. She says it clouds and complicates both their acting and the production itself. But, as in A Midsummer Night's Dream, actors continued to fall for each other. They just did it in secret. Rather like Hermia and Lysander in the play. Hermia's father wanted her to marry Demetrius and threatened her with death if she continued her relationship with Lysander. You see, when we manipulate people, death sometimes results."

Someone from the floor called up, "That's all very interesting, but we all know that Charlie from the bookshop got into it with Jeremy last night. They beat each other up over some girl and then Jeremy got killed. And Charlie was with the police all day. Sounds to me like that case has already been solved."

"Except that Charlie didn't kill Jeremy."

"No, I didn't," Charlie agreed from somewhere in the back.

My heckler silenced, I continued. "Liam. You told me, and then you told the police that you had seen Charlie climbing over the wall. What time was that?"

Since he and I had already talked this through his answer was ready. "I saw him come over the wall about midnight. He went back over about a quarter of an hour later."

"But that wasn't Charlie you saw coming back over the wall. You thought it was, because you'd see him come in. It was Miles." I looked back at Charlie and Alice. "You see, Charlie went out by the gate. You don't need a security code to leave the college at night, only to get in. Charlie was already feeling a bit sore from his fight, so he walked out of the college the easiest way he could."

Miles had been propping up the side wall with his shoulder, but from the moment I'd said I knew who the killer was, he'd gone rigid. I could feel his eyes burning holes through me even from that far away. Now he straightened and turned to face me, but he didn't say anything.

"One of the secret relationships in the real life drama was that between Miles Thompson and Sofia Bazzano. Except that it wasn't as secret as Miles had hoped. Several people mentioned to me that they had thought there was something going on there."

There was a buzz of agreement.

"And then Sofia disappeared."

Sofia's voice rang out. "That wasn't Miles. Miles would never hurt me. Tell her, Miles, tell her."

But he didn't say a word. He still stared at me.

"Sofia didn't get a very good part in the play. Neither did Will. They bumped into each other here having both received disappointing news. In fact, Ellen Barrymore told me that when Sofia challenged her about her tiny part she told Sofia that she'd never make it as an actress." I gazed out at Sofia. "Sofia? Is that true?"

"Yes! She told me it was pointless to continue. I had no talent. With my pretty face, I might be able to do a bit of modeling, but I should give up any hopes of acting."

Murmurs went through the crowd. Ellen said, quite sharply, "Part of my job is to be honest with my actors. If I let her believe she had potential it would only break her heart later. I wanted to save her the pain."

"However, Sofia was very upset when she left here. She bumped into Will and he invited her for a drink at the pub. And then she disappeared."

"I was kidnapped," Sofia called out, as though I might have forgotten.

"Wait a minute," Will yelled out. "I didn't have anything to do with it. I only invited her for a drink."

I ignored the interruption. "Sofia arrived back today with this strange story that she'd been kidnapped. She had no idea by whom. There was no ransom demand. She wasn't hurt in any way. But she woke up yesterday out of a drugged state to find herself in a tiny village almost at the border with Scotland. Fortunately for her, she found some nice people who helped her get home. But you made one phone call, Sofia, didn't you?"

"Yes."

"Who did you phone, Sofia?"

"Miles. He wasn't there. I've told you already. I didn't get to talk to him, because he wasn't there."

"No. But you left him a message, didn't you?"

"Of course I did. I knew he'd be sick with worry. So I left a voice message telling him what had happened to me and that I was on my way home."

"That was last night. Sofia got the overnight train and

arrived in Oxford this morning." I looked down at her. "When you saw Miles today, the only person you wanted to phone yesterday, the person you'd come all the way back from Scotland to see, how did he react?"

Her shoulders slumped. "Weird."

"In fact, I was standing right there. He repulsed you. He tried to get you to go home and stay away, didn't he?"

"Yes," she said sounding upset.

I looked at him. "Why, Miles?"

He stared at me through slitted eyes, a sullen expression seeming to glue his lips together. I let the silence build but he didn't say anything.

I tried another tack. I could feel sweat building under my armpits. This impromptu one-woman show was getting me nowhere.

"Last night at the pub, Miles and Liam were joking around and did a whole scene of A Midsummer Night's Dream as though they were Welsh miners."

"Bloody cheek," I heard Daffyd say.

"In order to check the lines, Miles pulled out his script. Do you remember that, Miles?"

He still said nothing.

"Scarlett, you remember, don't you?"

"Yes."

"So, witnesses can put you and that script in the pub before the murder. But where was that script found today?"

Scarlett spoke up again. "It was on the stage, near where Jeremy's body was."

"Scarlett, are you absolutely positive that was Miles's script?"

"Yes. He wrote his phone number on the corner of it and

tore it off to give it to me. I recognized the way it was torn. Also, he'd highlighted his own sections of speech. It was definitely his script that I saw in the evidence bag today."

I looked down at Miles. "So, Miles, how did your script get onto the stage between the time Jeremy was last seen alive and when he was found dead?"

Finally, he unglued his lips and spoke. "You have all the answers, you tell me?"

"There are two possibilities. Either you dropped it on the stage, possibly when you were murdering your good friend —" I was interrupted by a scream, which I thought came from Sofia. I waited for the noise to pass. "Or, someone planted it there to make you look guilty."

There were gasps of shock and I heard someone begin to cry. The people closest to Miles began to edge away as though being in proximity to him might put them in danger. All except Rafe, who moved a step closer. If Miles tried to run, he wouldn't get far.

I kept staring at Miles and he stared back. He was a tougher nut to crack than I had hoped. I continued, "Earlier today I overheard you say that it was your fault that Jeremy was dead. What did you mean by that?"

"If you're so sure I killed my mate, get your copper friends to arrest me."

I shook my head. "Miles, can't you see that it's over? None of the dreams you sacrificed yourself for are going to come true now."

"You don't know that," he said almost in a croak.

"How dare you say that to him," Ellen said, running up towards Miles. "He's the most talented student I've ever taught."

She grew closer to her prized pupil and he flinched away. "Don't touch me," he cried out in horror.

Sylvia had wanted me to push until a mask fell away. I wished she could be here and see how effectively I had just done that. When Ellen's mask fell away I saw the raw pain and longing in her face as she looked at Miles.

I said, "Miles was your way back into the limelight, wasn't he? This young, beautiful man with all that talent and potential. You groomed him, taught him everything you knew about acting, loved him."

She shook her head. "That's not true." But everything about her, from her face to her demeanor suggested that it was true. She turned to Miles and put out her hands in appeal. "Miles. Tell them it's not true."

He backed away from her until his back hit the wall. "Why?" he asked. "Why did you kill him? He was no threat to us."

There was a beat of painful silence. I've often heard the expression you could hear a pin drop. In this case, the silence was so intense I heard the flame on one of the candles sputter. I said, "But he was a threat. Jeremy had a secret. He told a couple of people that his ship had come in. He was going to get his big break as an actor. He didn't describe it as a dream or goal, but as though it were an actual, definite fact."

"I told you he was full of confidence," Ellen said. She was trying to pull her dignity back around her, but it was seriously frayed at the edges.

"Some of his friends thought he had landed an agent, or won a juicy role. But, that wasn't it, was it, Ellen? He'd seen you and Miles together, hadn't he? Did he blackmail you? Threaten to tell the board of governors about your affair with a student if you didn't promise him a plum role in your first production as the artistic director of Neptune Theatre? Perhaps he wanted more. Introductions to agents."

She stood frozen, as though she couldn't decide what to say, or do.

"He wouldn't have wanted money, he had plenty of that. He wanted something money couldn't buy. Something you could give him. That lucky break."

She pointed a shaking finger at me. "How dare you. How dare you make these terrible accusations? You have no proof."

"Miles?" I looked at him. "Tell us the truth. You owe it to Jeremy. You owe it to Sofia." Finally, I said, "You owe it to yourself."

He gripped his hair with his hands, bending forward as though he couldn't hold in the truth any longer. "It was just a bit of fun, at first, sleeping with the hot, older teacher. Of course we had to keep it all secret. There'd have been hell to pay if anyone found out. So, we were careful. That was half the fun."

"No. Miles," Ellen said.

He ignored her and looked up at me. "You're right. She promised me I could have any role I wanted. She promised to make me a star. I didn't know that staying with her was part of the deal. We were going to be a power couple, that's what she said."

Ellen was weeping now. "We'd have taken London by storm."

"I tried to end it, but she said she loved me. I didn't know what to do. She'd been so good to me, giving me extra help, mentoring me."

"When did you realize how dangerous she was?"

Miles looked about him, searching for someone. "When Sofia went missing. Ellen never said in so many words that she was behind it, but she let me know that if I promised to stay with her and never to see Sofia again, nothing would happen to the girl. So I promised."

What a bargain with the devil.

"I thought that would be it. But then, I don't know, she got worse. More clingy, more possessive."

"No! Miles, you love me. We love each other."

He shook his head. "Get away from me. You're disgusting."

I said, "It was you Liam saw climbing over the wall to leave the college after midnight last night, wasn't it?"

He nodded. "Sofia had called and left a message. I knew she was coming back here. I wanted to make sure Ellen wouldn't do anything crazy. So I went to her house." His voice croaked. "She was pacing up and down when I got there. She told me Jeremy had seen us together and would tell everyone if she didn't promise him the same opportunities she'd promised me."

"I tried to calm her down. I said he only wanted a leg up, and she'd been planning to give it to him anyway."

His shoulders began to shake and when he spoke, it was through tears. "I said I'd talk to him but she said, no. She'd do it."

"And so, Ellen, you asked Jeremy to meet you here. I'm guessing you played along with his demands, gave him a private lesson on the big stage, nice and early this morning before anyone was around. You met in secret with him, as you had with Miles, so he wasn't suspicious."

"No," Ellen moaned. "It wasn't like that."

"You let him put on a cape and flourish his wooden

sword. And then you picked up one of the stones and, when his back was turned, you killed him."

"No."

"You knew Miles would guess immediately who'd killed his friend, and so you added an insurance policy. You dropped Miles's script near the body. You must have taken it when he'd visited you last night. By planting evidence that he could have murdered Jeremy, you were sending him a message. Weren't you?"

"There was no evidence Miles had killed Jeremy. I knew he wouldn't be arrested."

"But he'd be frightened. Of you. And do whatever you wanted."

"I did everything for you, Miles. For us!"

She reached for him and he ran, right onto the stage. I thought he was going to take the microphone and so I stepped back to give him access but instead he said, "I'm sorry," and then ran to the back of the stage.

Ellen followed him calling out his name and rushed past me, too. She looked wild-eyed and crazed.

"Fire exit," I heard Rafe call out. How had I not known there was another exit? I didn't know what Ellen planned, or if she had any kind of weapon with her, but I couldn't leave Miles with her out there alone. I followed. Rafe shouted, "Lucy, no." But, I didn't listen.

Behind the stage was a network of corridors. I ran along a dark tunnel-like hallway and then down a set of stairs to the door. I flung it open and ran outside. The cold hit me immediately. It wasn't late, not even six o'clock, but it was already dark, and some sort of fog or mist had settled among the ancient trees. For the door let out into the ancient forest planted so many hundreds of years ago.

There was dim lighting meant to guide the students to their dorms, but it focused on the paths, leaving the treed areas in darkness and what light there was, had become obscured and murky because of the mist. I called out, "Miles. Ellen. There's no point running. The police will find you."

I heard a twig crack and ran forward. I thought, blindly, that if I could spot Miles I could put a protection spell on him. I tried to anyway, but my mind was a jumble and I was having trouble concentrating. Ellen's feelings were too raw. Her pain and longing and anguish had crept inside me and I couldn't push past them. So I tried to appeal to her. "Ellen. You don't want to hurt Miles. You love him."

I could hear footsteps, now, and voices crying out. I saw Miles run across the path, illuminated briefly, and then Ellen following behind. I caught the gleam of something in her hand. It took me a second to realize it was a small and very ladylike looking pistol. I ran for her, I don't really know what I thought I was going to do, but before I reached her, I was pushed bodily out of the way and sprawled to the ground.

I cried out in pain as I hit the root of an ancient tree. Ian had pushed past me and sprinted past, then, as I watched, he threw his body forward, catching Ellen in a rugby tackle.

I heard the clatter as they fell. People were running everywhere, calling. There was chaos. My head was ringing.

"Take my hand," the cool, calm voice said. I looked up and there was Rafe. I reached up and took his hand and he pulled me to my feet. "Are you hurt?"

I shook my head.

He looked me up and down as though to make sure and

then slipped the jacket from his shoulders. "Here. You're cold."

I put his jacket on gratefully even as I said, "It's your coat. Won't you be cold?"

His smile was mocking. "I never feel the cold."

Of course he didn't. My poor brain was addled.

I heard Ian reading Ellen her rights as he arrested her for Jeremy's murder. Two uniformed officers ran past. And so did Sofia who kept calling Miles's name.

"Sofia." It was Miles, answering. While I watched, he came forward and took her in his arms. "I'm so sorry," he said in a broken voice. "I tried to break it off with her. I never meant for any of this to happen."

"I know," she said.

"Can you ever forgive me?"

"Probably. But you should've told me."

"I know I should have. I promise, there will never be any secrets between us again."

He led her back towards the dorm rooms and, as they passed, Rafe said in a low voice, "And that promise will last about five minutes."

I couldn't help but laugh. "Are you really that cynical about love?"

"No. Quite the contrary. But men and women should have secrets from each other." He looked at me. "Would you really want to know all my secrets?"

I shuddered at the thought. "No. Definitely not."

"And, if a man you cared for wanted to surprise you with a gift, or a weekend away, perhaps, would you really want to know in advance? Or would you want him to keep it a secret?"

"All right. I take your point. All secrets aren't bad ones."

Two uniformed officers led a weeping Ellen past us. She was in handcuffs.

Ian followed more slowly. He was limping. "Ian, are you all right?" I asked.

He looked at me and nodded. "Old football injury." He looked confused and a little sad. "Lucy," he began, and then he shook his head. "I owe you an explanation, but I don't have one. I'm sorry. I've got to get to the station now. I'll call you later. We'll talk."

"All right."

He was about to walk on and then turned back to me. "How were you so certain it was Ellen?"

I thought about it. "I think it was Shakespeare who showed me the way. The extraordinary lengths and cruelties that people go to in the name of love." I looked around the ancient college buildings and the old trees still indistinct in the mist. "She desperately wanted to get back in the limelight. Here, she had power and then she fell hard for Miles, her beautiful young man."

I shrugged. "When you mix love and power together they can be a deadly combination. I remember when I first looked Ellen up online and saw those pictures of her at the height of her fame. They were reminders of her glory days. Every day, when she worked with the next generation of actors, she was reminded of how far she felt she had fallen. I believe she was obsessed with getting back onto center-stage, and Miles was her ticket.

"Perhaps she really did love him, but she used him as well. And what he thought was simply an affair with a beautiful, older woman, and his teacher, was something very different for her. When it became clear that he didn't see the two of them going forward as a power couple, taking London by storm, I think something in her snapped. When she realized that he preferred a fellow student to the great Ellen Barrymore it was too much."

He leaned down to rub his knee. "And you're certain that she was behind Sofia Bazzano's kidnapping?"

"Yes." I knew Rafe would not want to be involved, even though he was the one who had spotted the kidnapper. "I bet if you look at the CCTV footage from the pub after Will left Sofia, you'll find that someone close to Ellen slipped a drug into her drink."

"Close to Ellen? You mean she hired someone to do this?"

"I'd start with Alex Blumstein." The woman was stocky, tough, and had worked with Ellen for years. "She and Ellen go way back. I have a feeling she'd do anything for her boss."

He nodded again. "Good work. I'll call you."

Then he limped away.

After he was out of earshot, Rafe said, "Don't you have a recipe for a special tea that would take the detective inspector's aches and pains away?"

I shuddered and pulled the edges of his jacket closer. "Yes, I do. And I am never feeding a magical potion to a human ever again."

He chuckled softly. "Nonsense. But, I admit, he deserves to suffer."

After the way Ian had stood me up for our fancy date, and made a fool of himself over Scarlett, I privately agreed.

I was warm now with Rafe's jacket around me. Everyone had gone back in so we seemed to be alone in this ancient wood. Moonlight gilded the aged trees and lit up the mist so it looked like wisps of lace.

I was in no hurry to go back inside to where there'd be more police, more questions. That would come soon enough, but I needed a minute. The moon was no longer full, but beginning to fade.

"It's beautiful out here," I said.

"Yes," Rafe answered. "In a play about love blindness, Ellen was suffering from it, herself. Rather appropriate that her final scene should play out in a magic wood, just like in the play."

"I suppose I'll have to finish reading the play now to find out how it ends."

Rafe chuckled softly. "The play ends, very appropriately, with the correct lovers back together and the magical creatures finished playing games with mere mortals."

"It seems wrong of magical creatures to toy with mortals for sport."

He looked down at me and his eyes glittered. "Not always for sport. Sometimes, perhaps, the creature longs for one moment of happiness to take with him into his eternal future."

My heart was beginning to pound. "Is it ever enough?"

His smile was wry. "Better, I think, than no happiness at all."

"And what of the mortal? Does she always have no memory of what happened in the magical wood?"

"That is up to her."

And then he kissed me.

A Note from Nancy

Dear Reader,

Thank you for reading the Vampire Knitting Club series. I am so grateful for all the enthusiasm this series has received. I have plenty more stories about Lucy and her undead knitters planned for the future.

I hope you'll consider leaving a review and please tell your friends who like cozy mysteries.

Review on Amazon, Goodreads or BookBub.

Your support is the wool that helps me knit up these yarns.

Until next time,
Happy Reading,

Nancy

THE GREAT WITCHES BAKING SHOW

Excerpt from Prologue

Elspeth Peach could not have conjured a more beautiful day. Broomewode Hall glowed in the spring sunshine. The golden Cotswolds stone manor house was a Georgian masterpiece, and its symmetrical windows winked at her as though it knew her secrets and promised to keep them. Green lawns stretched their arms wide, and an ornamental lake seemed to welcome the swans floating serene and elegant on its surface.

But if she shifted her gaze just an inch to the left, the sense of peace and tranquility broke into a million pieces. Trucks and trailers had invaded the grounds, large tents were already in place, and she could see electricians and carpenters and painters at work on the twelve cooking stations. As the star judge of the wildly popular TV series *The Great British Baking Contest,* Elspeth Peach liked to cast her discerning eye over the setup to make sure that everything was perfect.

When the reality show became a hit, Elspeth Peach had been rocketed to a household name. She'd have been just as happy to be left alone in relative obscurity, writing cookbooks and devising new recipes. When she'd first agreed to judge amateur bakers, she'd imagined a tiny production watched only by serious foodies, and with a limited run. Had she known the show would become an international success, she never would have agreed to become so public a figure. Because Elspeth Peach had an important secret to keep. She was an excellent baker, but she was an even better witch.

Elspeth had made a foolish mistake. Baking made her happy, and she wanted to spread some of that joy to others. But she never envisaged how popular the series would become or how closely she'd be scrutinized by The British Witches Council, the governing body of witches in the UK. The council wielded great power, and any witch who didn't follow the rules was punished.

When she'd been unknown, she'd been able to fudge the borders of rule-following a bit. She always obeyed the main tenet of a white witch—do no harm. However, she wasn't so good at the dictates about not interfering with mortals without good reason. Now, she knew she was being watched very carefully, and she'd have to be vigilant. Still, as nervous as she was about her own position, she was more worried about her brand-new co-host.

Jonathon Pine was another famous British baker. His cookbooks rivaled hers in popularity and sales, so it shouldn't have been a surprise that he'd been chosen as her co-judge. Except that Jonathon was also a witch.

She'd argued passionately against the council's decision

to have him as her co-judge, but it was no good. She was stuck with him. And that put the only cloud in the blue sky of this lovely day.

To her surprise, she saw Jonathon approaching her. She'd imagined he'd be the type to turn up a minute before cameras began rolling. He was an attractive man of about fifty with sparkling blue eyes and thick, dark hair. However, at this moment he looked sheepish, more like a sulky boy than a baking celebrity. Her innate empathy led her to get right to the issue that was obviously bothering him, and since she was at least twenty years his senior, she said in a motherly tone, "Has somebody been a naughty witch?"

He met her gaze then. "You know I have. I'm sorry, Elspeth. The council says I have to do this show." He poked at a stone with the toe of his signature cowboy boot—one of his affectations, along with the blue shirts he always wore to bring out the color of his admittedly very pretty eyes.

"But how are you going to manage it?"

"I'm hoping you'll help me."

She shook her head at him. "Five best-selling books and a consultant to how many bakeries and restaurants? What were you thinking?"

He jutted out his bottom lip. "It started as a bit of a lark, but things got out of control. I became addicted to the fame."

"But you know we're not allowed to use our magic for personal gain."

He'd dug out the stone now with the toe of his boot, and his attention dropped to the divot he'd made in the lawn. "I know, I know. It all started innocently enough. This woman I met said no man can bake a proper scone. Well, I decided to show her that wasn't true by baking her the best scone she'd ever tasted. All right, I used a spell, since I couldn't bake a scone or anything else, for that matter. But it was a matter of principle. And then one thing led to another."

"Tell me the truth, Jonathon. Can you bake at all? Without using magic, I mean."

A worm crawled lazily across the exposed dirt, and he followed its path. She found herself watching the slow, curling brown body too, hoping. Finally, he admitted, "I can't boil water."

She could see that the council had come up with the perfect punishment for him by making the man who couldn't bake a celebrity judge. He was going to be publicly humiliated. But, unfortunately, so was she.

He groaned. "If only I'd said no to that first book deal. That's when the real trouble started."

Privately, she thought it was when he magicked a scone into being. It was too easy to become addicted to praise and far too easy to slip into inappropriate uses of magic. One bad move could snowball into catastrophe. And now look where they were.

When he raised his blue eyes to meet hers, he looked quite desperate. "The council told me I had to learn how to bake and come and do this show without using any magic at all." He sighed. "Or else."

"Or else?" Her eyes squinted as though the sun were blinding her, but really she dreaded the answer.

He lowered his voice. "Banishment."

She took a sharp breath. "As bad as that?"

He nodded. "And you're not entirely innocent either, you

know. They told me you've been handing out your magic like it's warm milk and cuddles. You've got to stop, Elspeth, or it's banishment for you, too."

She swallowed. Her heart pounded. She couldn't believe the council had sent her a message via Jonathon rather than calling her in themselves. She'd never used her magic for personal gain, as Jonathon had. She simply couldn't bear to see these poor, helpless amateur bakers blunder when she could help. They were so sweet and eager. She became attached to them all. So sometimes she turned on an oven if a baker forgot or saved the biscuits from burning, the custard from curdling. She'd thought no one had noticed.

However, she had steel in her as well as warm milk, and she spoke quite sternly to her new co-host. "Then we must make absolutely certain that nothing goes wrong this season. You will practice every recipe before the show. Learn what makes a good crumpet, loaf of bread and Victoria sponge. You will study harder than you ever have in your life, Jonathon. I will help you where I can, but I won't go down with you."

He leveled her with an equally steely gaze. "All right. And you won't interfere. If some show contestant forgets to turn their oven on, you don't make it happen by magic."

Oh dear. So they *did* know all about her little intervention in Season Two.

"And if somebody's caramelized sugar starts to burn, you do not save it."

Oh dear. And that.

"Fine. I will let them flail and fail, poor dears."

"And I'll learn enough to get by. We'll manage, Elspeth."

The word banishment floated in the air between them like the soft breeze.

"We'll have to."

Order your copy today! *The Great Witches Baking Show* is Book 1 in the series.

Vampire Knitting Club

The Vampire Book Club

The Vampire Book Club - Book 1

Chapter and Curse - Book 2

A Spelling Mistake - Book 3

The Great Witches Baking Show

The Great Witches Baking Show - Book 1

Baker's Coven - Book 2

A Rolling Scone - Book 3

A Bundt Instrument - Book 4

Toni Diamond Mysteries

Toni is a successful saleswoman for Lady Bianca Cosmetics in this series of humorous cozy mysteries. Along with having an eye for beauty and a head for business, Toni's got a nose for trouble and she's never shy about following her instincts, even when they lead to murder.

Frosted Shadow - Book 1

Ultimate Concealer - Book 2

Midnight Shimmer - Book 3

A Diamond Choker For Christmas - A Toni Diamond Mysteries Novella

The Almost Wives Club

An enchanted wedding dress is a matchmaker in this series of romantic comedies where five runaway brides find out who the best men really are!

The Almost Wives Club: Kate - Book 1

Second Hand Bride - Book 2

Bridesmaid for Hire - Book 3

The Wedding Flight - Book 4

If the Dress Fits - Book 5

Take a Chance series

Meet the Chance family, a cobbled together family of eleven kids who are all grown up and finding their ways in life and love.

Kiss a Girl in the Rain - Book 1

Iris in Bloom - Book 2

Blueprint for a Kiss - Book 3

Every Rose - Book 4

Love to Go - Book 5

The Sheriff's Sweet Surrender - Book 6

The Daisy Game - Book 7

Chance Encounter - Prequel

Take a Chance Box Set - Prequel and Books 1-3

For a complete list of books, check out Nancy's website at nancywarren.net

ABOUT THE AUTHOR

Nancy Warren is the USA Today Bestselling author of more than 70 novels. She's originally from Vancouver, Canada, though she tends to wander and has lived in England, Italy and California at various times. While living in Oxford she dreamed up The Vampire Knitting Club. She's currently in Bath, UK, where she often pretends she's Jane Austen. Or at least a character in a Jane Austen novel. Favorite moments include being the answer to a crossword puzzle clue in Canada's National Post newspaper, being featured on the front page of the New York Times when her book Speed Dating launched Harlequin's NASCAR series, and being nominated three times for Romance Writers of America's RITA award. She has an MA in Creative Writing from Bath Spa University. She's an avid hiker, loves chocolate and most of all, loves to hear from readers! The best way to stay in touch is to sign up for Nancy's newsletter at www.nancywarren.net.

To learn more about Nancy and her books
www.nancywarren.net

CPSIA information can be obtained
at www.ICGtesting.com
Printed in the USA
LVHW010210211221
706819LV00009B/563